HARROWING HAMLET

Angela Patmore

Published in 2014 by FeedARead.com Publishing

A CIP catalogue record for this title is available from the British Library.

Chapter One

Helen Constance Smith could breath. She lay there in the miracle of being alive and ate with her eyes. Everything was keen and vivid to her. She was seven but very much older. She noticed things. As though by some intelligent design, the raindrops, dotted with light, skiddered and slanted down the tall window opposite. They were dashing their little lives together, racing and dancing. Make a note, she thought.

That's when she had become a writer.

The row of windows had no curtains. She could see the handsome night. The long ward with its two regimental ranks of facing white linen beds was lit by a single lamp suspended low over the nurses' work station. Her bed was somewhere in the middle so she could see their table without moving her head. It was covered with a leaf green cloth and strewn with their books, as these were students. Periodically a nurse would get up to attend a moan. Her shoes squeaked as they crossed the scrubbed and polished wooden floor. Apart from that, and the odd snore: silence.

She was alive. That was the main thing. She had to take everything in, because it was all so beautiful, and it all made sense. She had got through the asthma again. She didn't need to sleep. She was too excited at being allowed to breath. No oxygen tent. No rubber mask strapped over her nose and mouth, no inhalers, no injections of pure adrenaline that made dents in the muscles of her skinny legs. Just the glorious air around her, going in and out of her with the rhythm of all life – 'so shall I never die', she thought. Peristalsis - lungs, digestion, heart, the tide, the stars. When you are alive, you notice connections.

No hallucinations either. The one about going down an ever narrowing tunnel was the most terrifying. It might have been a visual representation of what was going on in her small body. After days and nights of wheezing and fighting, her bronchial tubes were closing up. She was slowly suffocating. She lost control of all her bodily functions as she was being lifted into the ambulance, and she could hear the clangour of the vehicle's sirens as it sped through the London night towards Whipps Cross hospital. They cried out for her and she knew what they said. Make way, child about to die. While inside, the patient gasped and gagged.

This was better. This was breathing. Everybody else seemed to be able to do it without much thought. Hell, they weren't even grateful. The writer was though.

***

Inside the busy *Sunday News* offices, banks of monitors were alight. Fingers rippled gently over some of the luckier keyboards while index fingers plugged away at others. Phones sang, text messages blinked, conversations hummed. The journalists' faces, lit by monitors, scanned events with narrow eyes, ravening after news. Today, on Stencie Smith's desk, there was some. Her screen flickered with business: internet stories carrying mug shots of actor Declan Mahoney:

> *DEMENTED DECLAN DOES IT AGAIN*
>
> *Controversial Irish actor Declan Mahoney, 42, is in trouble with the law again after allegedly carrying a dagger into one of London's top eateries. Mahoney told shocked fellow-diners at the Wolseley brasserie in Piccadilly that the 15-inch stainless steel Irish ring dagger was for cutting up his steak. Appearing before magistrates…*
>
> *BIG DEC'S BIG CAT*
>
> *Some actors employ body guards. Declan Mahoney doesn't bother. The Irish star's pet Timber wolf 'Stillbad' accompanies him on the set of his latest….*

Stencie's career space was suddenly invaded by a stubbled chin next to her ear. Lisle Mayhew, 51, features editor, was ratting round her again, peering into her monitor, his eyes like small black beads.

'Can you nail him Stence? His Hamlet goes into production at the Theatre Royal next week. I'd love to get this bastard undressed.'

'What am I? Witchfinder General?'

'Do it for me, you cow. He shut some tabloid prat's finger in his car window and thinks he can do as he likes with the press.'

'Supposing he breaks my nose and licks it.'

'That'd do us'.

Mayhew often seemed to leer.

Stencie said nothing but puffed up at her mauve and black fringe. She used to be very fiery with men but had learned late in her thirties to act more matey. If only God had made her a lesbian. *She will have to look after her laptop on this one,* ran her interior monologue. Indeed, Mayhew's old reporter nostrils detected neat pheromones in the air.

'This bloke would do it in the street and frighten the horses. Bit of a stud, so I hear. So get down there and flash your nuds at him.'

My nuds? thought Stence, appalled. *How little progress has been made by serious female writers seeking to climb the greasy pole in journalism. Shit*, she thought. *Strike that.*

***

Stencie's enormous greyhound, Craig, lounged in the back of her fading old Mercedes as she bulleted down the M11. He had the entire back seat given over to his needs, the foot wells stuffed with pillows and blankets. Greyhounds are not renowned for sense and Craig had been known to fall off the seat at speed and lodge himself upside down, his spindly legs sprouting above him like plant shoots. So now he had his bed in the back, wanting only a punka wallah with a fan.

His owner's morning had screwed up. The village church sent someone from door to door rattling an urgent appeal tin just as she was leaving for work. Apparently whilst two or three were not gathered together, the roof had somehow lost its lead and leaked all over the pulpit.

Stencie, not of the faith, *was* a devout observer of stained glass. She had been to St Chapelle as a child and stood transfixed in its hall of hypnotic windows: a small asthmatic girl in a prism of blue and red light. She invited the young woman in while she searched her purse. *No blasted change.* Irritated, she scrawled a cheque and handed it over. The young acolyte was quick, spotting the match between the signatory and the name on a small pile of books on Stencie's kitchen table.

'Did you write all those?'

'Much good may it do me.'

'So how come I've never heard of you?'
As a professional, Stencie suffered a lot of public innocence.

On the motorway the windscreen began to spot with rain and a bright butterfly became caught in one of the wipers, its fight for life distracting her as she drove. Stence wanted to free it but couldn't, and her mind refused to go past its tiny crisis.

Rolling down the driver side window she leaned forward and reached out into the rain, trying to catch the wiper as it switched towards her right hand, the other dragging on the steering.

Everything lurched smartly left. Horns blared, Craig leapt up in fright and the car slurred over, ending up on the hard shoulder as the brakes bit down.

Stence sat there in shock. It took a few moments to absorb what had happened. Her heart thudded as she blew up at her fringe.

The cardinal is dead

The wipers still flashed back and forth, spraying the fine rain and freeing the lifeless butterfly, flinging it back out into nature whence it came.

The writer was visualising the words. Sometimes she had to dig for them and haul them to the surface, and this was the jobbing side of her work, editing and revising, knocking sentences together, cutting and pasting in a rush. '*Give me the deadline and I'll give you the article'* was the motto of Stencie's clan. Hacks were called hacks because they chopped and sliced their copy to order. But sometimes for no apparent reason the words came unbidden in a clear stream like this and announced themselves in her head. All she had to do then was to write them down. Purple passages for free, because these lines were evidently not her work at all. All arts professionals stood on the edge of this mystery, and like every one of them, Stencie had a theory of how it worked.

The cardinal is dead
And the red admiral

The strange words were written by *Alph*. This was what she called the power of inspiration that took the pen from the writer's bungling hand and - in the nanosecond between two ordinary thoughts - *wrote*. Whereas a writer might waste her life and labour for hours on an important passage, *Alph* took no time at all to come up with the goods. *Alph* had the authentic voice of authority. *Alph* was the author of anything of merit or originality that the writer ever produced. Authentic, authority, author. When a person is alive she notices such connections.

The words that came in the car were nothing whatever to do with Stence and yet she recognised them. She had never even thought of 'censors', the smoking ornamental chalices bearing incense that swung during high church services, but she received the image of them swinging back and forth like windscreen wipers.

The cardinal is dead
and the red admiral with his glass windows
shivered particles of promises
and prayers which would not fail.
Censors swung smoking like the
switch of an angry tail
as shadows of gothic shoulders
shrank in the cathedral gloom,
a dark mass lowering its head
not daring to presume
to pray in the silent wake
of the dead cardinal.

Where did that come from? Stence sat in the driver's seat scribbling these new words down. She always did, wherever they occurred, and indeed she felt under some compulsion to do so.

She examined the phrases, the metaphors, and how they knitted together with their own internal logic. So far as she knew they were not quoted or borrowed, yet they were certainly not crafted by her. Nor were they of any practical relevance that she could see.

She herself was on a mission to interview a barking Irish actor, one who 'bore on his brow the mark of the fire from heaven'. That phrase was definitely not hers either, though it stuck fast in her head.

Chapter Two

The façade of the Corn Exchange, Tunbridge Wells was imprisoned in scaffolding. The august building, although it had suffered all the insults of time and pollution and was looking a little rough hewn round the edges, had done nothing wrong. Indeed, before it was transformed from Mrs Sarah Baker's Tunbridge Wells Theatre into the more practical building of today, it had seen some remarkable productions. The Regency tragedian Edmund Kean performed there, holding his audiences spellbound with his demonic genius.

Now the dilapidated Exchange was undergoing a radical refit, and two Irish double glazing fitters were working hard on the upstairs windows beneath the roof.

Reaching into an opening, one of them pulled out assorted rubbish, curiously examining what people long departed may have thrown away.

Among the detritus was something quite remarkable. He turned it over in his hands. It appeared to be a child's threadbare toy. What it represented was anyone's guess. An animal of some kind: a dog, perhaps, or a pig. Its ears were set high on its head so it might even have been a bear.

'Would you ever look at that! I reckon that's something', exclaimed the finder, his cigarette stub glued for safety to his lower lip.

'Show us it here. Where the devil did that come from?' asked his mate.
The first fitter gestured.

'That'll be old. I reckon that's old. They're worth a bit, them things.'

'Would that be Roosevelt's first teddy, do you think?' the first fitter queried, admiring his own Celtic wit.

'Was he Victorian? Looks older than that, doesn't it. Would you give us a hand with this then?'

The first fitter stuffed the antique in his belt, and the two men positioned themselves at either end of a loose scaffolding plank, bending down to lift it.

There was a long pause, and not because the plank was particularly heavy. At length the second fitter looked up. Something had suddenly marred the person that he was. His face and eyes were momentarily horrific.

His workmate, meeting his gaze, recoiled and stepped back, losing his footing. As he fell, he instinctively clutched at anything to hand, and his grip fastened on the window frame to save him. They were three floors up.

'Mother of God!'
His mate, who had mysteriously returned to normal, was amused.

'You mind how you go there, Sean!' The first fitter brushed himself down, and the bear fell on to the plank-work. The man picked it up, looking carefully at his workmate.

'He brought you luck, the little feller,' the face was saying.

'Mother of God.'

'Reckon you'll be taking that to Christies now. Few bob there.'

The finder had recovered his composure. We all seamlessly close our minds to what we fear, and this could all have been the lunchtime stout.

'Naw. I'll give it to my little lad. He likes that sort of thing.'

'Up we go then.'

They lifted the plank and carried it along the facade. The proud Corn Exchange said never a word about the incident. It had finally disgorged something not particularly to its liking.

***

Away in the window of a far different building, the Theatre Royal, Drury Lane, an aerial spy could just make out Julia Lord, well blonded and wearing large spider ear-rings and a T-shirt emblazoned with 'BURNS INC SUPPORTING SHAKESPEARE', racing into the dressing room she shared with her boyfriend.

With both hands, the actress was clutching an exotic bottle. It contained pure alcohol, it was not hers, and this was not a piece of stage business. Running towards the sink she unscrewed the cap in panic and was about to empty the contents down the plughole when she heard the ominous footsteps outside. Rescrewing the top, she stashed the hooch quickly in a wardrobe and sat at her dressing mirror, brushing her hair with a fury.

Yorkshireman John Padgett, pink-faced, plunged in the door, stopped dead and scanned the dressing room. His smile was handsome, narrow and slightly vicious. Lifting Julia out of her seat, he shook her back and forth.

'Give. Come on Julie, or I'll bloody smack you.'

'No. You promised me John. It's bad luck.'

Padgett, a not unreasonable fellow, resigned himself. It can't have gone far: he would find it later. However she had to learn, and he would tutor her: he always did.

'Oh *luck*. Bloody desperate Dan was at the theatre till 3 o'clock this morning with his paper cut-outs trying to re-do the blocking. Or re-re-do it. Gives you every confidence that bloke. Or the shits. I don't know whether I'm upstage without a paddle or downwind of brown trousers.'

'Dan' was director Daniel Loxley, and he ruled this theatre while he was in it with a rod of iron awe. They knew the man from academe was on his way to light fires under their backsides.

The pair were getting ready for an important 'sponsor's viewing' rehearsal, and while Julia hurried, John deliberately dawdled, trying to make them late. Stripping off her T-shirt to reveal the kind of female acting talent Padgett most admired, Julia was already fighting her way into a tight Elizabethan bodice. Their proper costumes weren't ready yet: they were merely improvising with hired gear, dressing up for some VIP called Harvey Burns II.

'Who *are* Burns Inc anyway?' she grunted.

'Do you mean to tell me you've never heard of Longhorns, the fags from Texas?'

'Oh that's great isn't it.'

It's worse than that,' Padgett said, sniffing some second-hand Shakespearean tights. 'The only reason Harvey Burns is bankrolling the production is because he's a cousin of our director's missus.'

'John?' Julia had still not finished doing up her bodice.

'Hallo.'

'Aren't I your little posh lass any more?' She held her burly Yorkshireman at arm's length and looked steadily into his face. Nothing was written on it.

Padgett was here playing Horatio but he might as well have been playing polo. He liked his sport, having been born within queuing distance of Headingley cricket ground. In fact, if required, young Padgett could show you a sound forward defensive stroke, the hallmark of Yorkshire cricket, preferring the great cricketing icons of that county to neurotic southerners, luvvies and pooftas. He was quite fond of Julia, but nothing unmanly.

'Any road', he responded without conceding a wicket, 'I thought we were shooting up to your mother's for a bit of partridge bloody pie.'

'She's sick, John. How many more times?'

'She'll be sicker yet when she comes to Opening Night and sees her daughter going (imitating Julia's very bad Ophelia): '*Young men will do't when they come to't, By Cock, they are to blame!*'

Julia did not retaliate. She was too crest-fallen for that. They both knew their overbearing director was to blame for her imploding performance and that she had bowed under repeated blows to her confidence.

Loxley was a tyrant and Julia objected to him. She was an innocent from a wealthy northern family and admired working class heroes like Padgett, whom she trusted as sterling and sane. In contrast her mother Coral, another sensitive creature of the stage, had turned red as a tomato from the radiotherapy yet still somehow nursed unrealistic hopes of everything including her daughter's career.

The younger Miss Lord was not vain or deluded. She knew she would never be famous. Ironically her very egolessness shielded her from dark forces ever at work in the theatre, where everybody else so longed to be a star. She reached into her pink leather handbag and showed her partner a small silver box containing Coral's good-luck gift to them for this production. And this production needed all the help it could get.

The rabbit's foot seemed to cast a shadow over her boyfriend's chiselled features. Glancing heavenward he flashed his hand sideways, snatched up the talisman and disappeared into their bathroom annex.

'Oh John! No! Please – oh you swine boy!' Julia screamed after him. The toilet door swung back and Padgett returned, wiping his large paws on a towel. Nor was he finished with the matter. 'Bloody luvvies' bloody rites and rituals all over the place. Bloody theatre superstitions. St Genesius that our James Mayne Young wears round his neck: poor dear, he was martyred by the Emperor Diocletian, Jamesie baby. The best place for his St

Genesius is up his arse, if there's any room left.' And he bellowed with laughter.

'Julia – watch this.'

In a loud, belligerent chant and standing close to her as he stamped his feet, Padgett delivered his treatise on their craft.

All acting is, is this!
On you go, you say your lines!
You have your fights!
Then off you come
And then you say
Where were the bollocking lights!
All the rest is crap!
Crap, crap, crap!
All right? ALL RIGHT?

Julia always tried to remain passive and pretty, even with doom in the air. 'I think James was married once. Please, John.'

'So? Bloody Tchaikovsky was bloody married. Sodding Oscar Wilde was sodding married.' Then, seeing his woman's lower lip possibly starting to wobble, Padgett relented and threw his arm round her.

'We'll get through it Julia. God's teeth! Zounds! We'll be all right. We're sponsored professionals. Journeymen and journeypersons. Besides, if anyone's going to take a pop at our Daniel, it's me. You know what he calls me, don't you.'

'What? *What?*' He had Julia smiling again.

'Declan told me. "Oh Padgett" he says, when they're casting Horatio between them – "*the boy with the rack of wooden winkles*". What does that mean? I mean, what does that mean?'

There was a loud banging on the door and a female voice yelled: 'FIVE MINUTES!'

'Shit!' chorused John and Julia.

***

Stence had left Craig in her car on double yellow lines in Drury Lane with all the windows down for air and would almost certainly get clamped. She ran up the steps and into the theatre, where she pushed her press pass under the nose of a receptionist in the booking hall.

'Where would I find Declan Mahoney's dressing room please?'

The receptionist owled at Stence without answering. Fans could always download or forge press passes these days. This looked like a fan, a little past her sell-by date but then Mahoney affected that generation as any other. He was in films, you know.

'I'm here to do an interview at eleven for the *Sunday News*.'

'Mr Mahoney isn't here', the woman sneared. 'You'll have to contact him at his hotel.'

'Thanks, I'll wait'.

'You can't wait here.'

'That's OK'.

Stence pushed open double doors leading into the inner sanctuary. The receptionist was already on the phone as the intruder made her way towards the auditorium. On the fiercely lit stage, rehearsals were underway as Stence ducked into a seat near the front, along the row from a sorrowful fat man in a pastel suit whose face circled an unlit cigar.

Stence's camera eyeballs panned the stage for the Great Man in case the receptionist had lied, but sure enough a large black hole gaped where charisma should have shone. Daniel Loxley had just stopped them in the middle of the Osric scene.

'Right, now every bugger come and sit down here!'

Loxley's Oxford accent was crisp and sharp. The famous director turned out to be a small but significant-looking balding man in his forties: Stence had never seen him before but she would have recognised him instantly. *Will Shakespeare went to Spec Savers*. She often thought in smartarse journalese while she was doing her job.

'Good,' Loxley continued. 'Now can we dim all the lights? Leave me a single spot centre stage? Thank you. Now I want silence, *as of the grave*.'

Stillness. Nothing stirred. Nobody moved. Nothing questioned the man in charge. As the lights tapered, Loxley's commanding voice resonated with the theatre's strange acoustics. It seemed to be casting a spell. Suddenly his pointing finger swept round and stabbed through the darkness at the small white circle on the stage.

'You see it? *There it is! – There!* You can't miss it once you look. *That*, children of the boards, is the famous Magic Spot, hushed up by generations of actors in fear, in hope, in reverence. I don't mean the point where that particular spotlight has landed. Of course not. I mean *the real one*. Because it's out there, *somewhere*. Paranormal, abnormal to secular audiences and critics, yet normal on a stage, in a theatre. How do you locate it, the Magic Spot? *You can't*. But if you give of your best, if you sacrifice yourself and you stand in that spot, wherever it happens to be, whenever it happens to be there, *something will occur to you. Ta-woo, woo-hoo-hoo-hoo!*' And the director hooted as he rippled his fingers over them. 'All right? Lights, thank you. Back here at 3pm sharp, watch the call sheet.'

The joyless fat man at the other end of Stence's row made a show of getting up and joining the cast as though he had some role in their fate. The actors began to disperse but the magic rather didn't. Stence could feel something mysterious in the air as she followed Julia and John out towards the dressing rooms. She wasn't yet ready to charm anything out of Loxley, but these two looked a softer touch so she walked awkwardly beside them. Padgett was speaking, as he usually was.

'Did I tell you Declan has been sniffed up by another sponsor for the digital TV movie of his *Tamburlaine*? Jammy....' He broke off, noticing a stranger present.

'Luck of the Irish', Julia shrugged.

The three of them had arrived at the dressing room before Stence introduced herself and confided her mission. It had all been agreed, but Mahoney was magnificently missing. He had been paid quite a tidy sum by the *Sunday News* as well. Padgett laughed.

'You'll be lucky,' he assured her. 'He hates journalists.'

'I'm not a hack. I'm a bloody writer.'

Stence spoke with probity but her expression showed any actor where it hurt, too. 'I do books but I have to scrape a living on features. I've never grassed out an interviewee yet', she smiled sadly and banged her old briefcase on her thigh. 'I couldn't in any case. Half my work is ghostwriting and I wouldn't get another contract. My success depends on having zipper lips. *Mmmmn-er-mmner.*' John smirked, but Julia actually giggled. They offered her a mug of Shiraz. And that was all she was likely to get on this trip.

Chapter Three

A metal bucket, distorted and squashed flat, lay on the gravel path between two rows of pink rhododendrons in the tiered ornamental gardens.

'Look at that,' said Harvey Burns II, pushing it with his sandaled foot. 'My guard dogs patrol the perimeter wall at night. German Shepherds you know, big as goddam donkeys. I got them from your RAF Police over here. They like to chew stuff.'

It was a 'no rehearsal day', a breather in the tight *Hamlet* schedule for the cast and crew, and Mr and Mrs Daniel Loxley were paying a visit to the play's beef baron sponsor at his modest British home. Sally Loxley, although not as rich as her cousin, had the family love of audacious living, and often stayed with 'her' Harvey when she was resting between parts and plastic surgery. The rolling hills of the 55-acre Burns estate were set in the magnificent Sussex Downs, screened on all sides by the Texan's lucrative conifer forests.

The property boasted state-of-the-art security. Harvey's winding drive bristled with small turrets and masts alert to anyone planning to 'maybe put a sawn off horse's head under a man's duvet', and the bust of Antoninus Pious that stared white-eyed across the croquet lawn was rumoured to listen in on staff cigarette breaks.

The heat was unseasonal for an April afternoon. By the pool Dan and Sally were sipping chilled Manhattens, trying to explain to sponsor

Harvey about his Big Mistake. You couldn't *not* have previews before a major London opening night. Previews gave the technical crews a chance to iron out little glitches and they gave the actors a dry run to work out their acts in front of a few live audiences.

'Otherwise the actors go out on First Night with their souls in their mouths,' Dan was saying.

'They're professionals, ain't they?' growled Harvey, his jowls glistening with sunblocker. 'If you have a good product, you don't show its ass to the market before you launch.'

'This isn't a *product,*' Dan argued. 'You can't go straight from dress rehearsals to First Night with a major play. Somebody's going to screw up. It's bloody dangerous.' Mrs Loxley leaned towards her cousin, revealing a magnificent set of plastic mammaries.

'This is how theatre works here, honey. It's not like the movies. In theatre they let the public in half-price for a few nights so the actors get a feel for the audience.'

'*Half-price?*' Harvey threw his sunglasses on the poolside table. 'I'm paying these actors big cheques, am I right?'

'You are,' sighed Dan.

'Good. So I'm not paying full price actors to do cut-price performances. *No previews*. Want another drink?'

And as Dan looked at Sally a sparkle of fear lit his eyes.

***

Craig was sprawled on the decking outside London's Bear Inn, a reference to the hostelry's glory days as an Elizabethan baiting venue. The bear in question would have fought for its life with bulldogs fastened to its flesh, their flattened layback muzzles allowing them to breath through the blood. Stence's own canine was fastened by his martingale to the leg of her chair.

Although she had her laptop with her, it was unopened and her mobile was switched off. She was in deep doodoo on the *Sunday News* features desk having failed to file, and was all alone here, staring into space, trying to clamber aboard her inner lifeboat when the man walked over.

He looked slightly dishevelled as though he had been in a scuffle. She feared he was about to ask for cash. Stence was far from flush and looked intently into her apple and watermelon drink. Craig looked up, though he had not a shred of guarding instinct and would have let his mistress be raped and robbed without demur before running off to save himself.

The man had a carrier bag with something in it. Not ready meals, by the shape.

'Excuse me,' he said in a Belfast brogue, caressing her with breath at least thirty per cent proof. 'Bot do you know the owner of dis establishment?' Stence thought of telling him to piss off.

'Of course. Gilbert and I are old friends.'

'That would be it then. Only I saw you had a lot of papers there,' the stranger smiled, revealing a full set of piano teeth. 'I thought maybe you worked for dis establishment.' He pronounced 'thought' *taught* and although Stence was on the lookout for an iconic Irishman, this was evidently not to be he.

'You see the ting is,' the fellow continued, 'I happen to have come by an antique, a valuable item that may be of interest to your friend the poblican.'

'Really? And what sort of item would that be?'

'It's a very rare steak – if you take my meaning.' And he actually winked. Stence looked in the bag anyway. A woollen scarf concealed the contents, which were drawn out with some ceremony by the owner and placed on the table next to her laptop. Unfurled, the priceless item was revealed to be a particularly dirty carved fur toy that fifty children might have knocked about. It attempted to be an animal of some kind.

'It's a *bear!*' announced the owner. 'And where do you tink it came from, dis little bear? Why, from the old Corn Exchange in Tunbridge Wells – de famous theatre dare! You see how it would enhance the *pob*', said the man, indicating the titular sign with his head. 'You could put it in a glass case. I could let you have it for as little as, say' (and here he lowered his voice) 'seventy.'

Stence hadn't had a lot of sleep lately and she felt her diaphragm begin to tickle. In a minute she would give way to open mirth.

'Wait here, I'll go and ask him,' she said. Stence went into the ladies taking her laptop, handbag and a slightly shocked Craig with her.

She was gone for some time, and when she came out the Irishman was getting into the back of a police car. It was not unexpected.

Her eyes followed the vehicle up the road and then came to rest on the carrier bag and its contents. As she was on her way back to the theatre she thought she might give the little bear his big break. Actors were superstitious after all, and this was an ancient theatre artefact. It was simply too good to miss. But as she bundled dog and baggage into the car, she did have a faint feeling of unease. *Butterflies. Please no more butterflies*.

We are often made to look small and mean by fate. Stence had been quite wrong about her Irish antique dealer. He was not an object of derision at all. Nor was he a small time criminal being arrested for petty theft. Sean Rafferty was an honest man, by trade a double glazing fitter. The police had come to find him because there had been a serious road traffic accident. His wife had crashed their car and his eight-year-old boy had been flung through the windscreen.

***

The greying actor, majestic in some hired velvet Claudius robes, leaned over the sink.

Unfortunately it was not his own sink. It belonged to John Padgett and his darling lady Julia. Padgett would not be thrilled to find James Mayne Young throwing up in his sink. In his view James was finished: 'it was only the costumes holding him up.' But James was taken ill there suddenly because he had recently stopped smoking and suffered from severe stage fright and angst spirals that gripped his stomach and forced its contents upwards.

As he leaned forward to retch, his lucky St Genesius pendant glimmered from his neck. He wore it always. Being of the old school, he was highly superstitious and would never say the tag lines of a play, or eat real food on the stage or name the Scottish tragedy.

James was now in his sixties and in the twilight of a distinguished career. He knew he was lucky to get this part and thanked God for it (being a late convert to Catholicism). It was a cruel pity that Loxley, whom he admired for his vast Shakespearean knowledge, already had his tyrant's knife in the man's back and blasphemed at him constantly during rehearsals. James had been out of work for two years, living in a bachelor pad following his divorce, and loneliness shadowed his life outside of the theatre. But he was still a commanding presence within it, his deep mellifluous voice effortlessly reaching all parts of the auditorium by sheer training and technique.

He used music to give him the clue to what actors call their tempo rhythms – the cadences of their breathing, emotions and speech patterns. For Claudius he had chosen Handel's *Messiah*, which accompanied him on an iPod wherever he strode. And stride he did, for James was a genuine king actor. Indeed, the man playing Claudius was from an old and very renowned acting family, one member having been a noted Regency performer, a rival of Edmund Kean.

Julia appeared, ever the lady, and thought only of giving the poor fellow a towel. She sat him down and mopped his face.

'Are you going to be OK? For a moment I thought you were our dictator.' James rallied under her kindness.

'Dan? Oh I've worked for worse.' Padgett had entered the room and his wit with him.

'Where was that, mate – the Coliseum?'

'Clever man, our Daniel. You're only seeing him under pressure here. I've never heard anybody discuss the magic of the theatre better than Daniel Loxley.'

'Man's a tithead', said Padgett, picking up the whiff of vomit.

'He's an ideas man, James', added Julia reluctantly. 'What we're short of in this country is bravura actors, not bravura directors.'

'Remember that talk he gave us about witchcraft in the theatre?' James offered, mopping his forehead with the towel. '*Wonderful* stuff.' By now Padgett was looking fairly dangerous.

'About actors being shamans and mediums?'

'Yes!'

'No. I don't remember it. I'm not interested in bloody superstitious bloody claptrap to explain away stage technique.'

'Oh *come on* old boy – the origins of the theatre are all to do with Orphic rites. It has religious significance. The ancient theatres of Japan are built on burial sites, did you know that?'

Padgett did not know that. Furthermore he was at his makeup, like the professional he was.

'No Kingie. Got any beard glue Kingie? I have to wear a bloody token beard with this get-up. Real costume still being made.'

Outside the door there was a sudden loud crashing noise, as though all the props were being overturned in a drug bust. The door flung open and Daniel Loxley, like an unexploded bomb, stood in its frame. His whole head appeared to be pulsing. His eyes were like twin coals. Immediately all the actors rose.

'*Why don't you fucking wastes of my time* get your fucking worthless arses out there for 3pm like I specifically re-fucking-quested? *YOU!*' he bellowed, indicating James. 'Wardrobe fitting room. *Right now*.' The robed king, completely cowed, got up and left immediately. '*You* mistress (indicating Julia) had better know your new turns and sing "Tomorrow is Saint Valentine's Day" without taking big breaths this afternoon or I'm going to flush you down the toilet. NICK!!!'

A stick-thin electrician appeared carrying a reel of transparent flex.

'Get in here! What's this doing in this dressing room?' Loxley's foot kicked at a piece of equipment on the floor. 'This is the other breezebox for the ghost scenes. Where's the first one? *I didn't hear you!*'

'I dunno.'

'Get out.' Nick, petrified, almost took the door with him.

'Julia, what's the matter now?'

'Tim borrowed it. Their dressing room is over the boiler room and he's got an –'

'For fuck *sake* what's the matter with this company. There's my Hamlet four sheets to the wind, there's Godsthorpe drying his bum on one of only two decent *Guster* units in this theatre and there's you, you stupid scrofulous *cow* with spots all over your face to play Hamlet's fucking heart's desire, strolling round half-dressed at half past two pm like some autistic toddler when as I never tire of telling you talentless twats *we're three days behind fucking schedule!* Julia, don't look at me like that, love.'

Padgett, having donned a black wig in the excitement, spoke up.

'We know we're under the hammer, Dan, there's no need to go off at a tangent. You're just making everybody nervous.'

Loxley, having looked almost maniacal, began to ease off.

'Ha ha! Nervous boy. I was here till three this morning, I don't know why I bother, moving all the blocking *back* for the scene in Gertrude's bedchamber because your seldom-seen designer friend has given me a fishnet curtain instead of an arras. Oh come on, Julia. You know I mean it. Anyway, it'll be my responsibility if this play goes plop, not yours. Cheer up, gel. Christ alive, John – take that off. You look like a Greek grannie. Come on, let's get it over with.'

And they all left the room, brimming with confidence that the production would be a tremendous success. Not surprisingly under the circumstances, none of them noticed a purple-haired writer standing outside with a press pass and a plastic bag.

Chapter Four

Stence's tiny rented cottage window was open, and a pink rose nodded in, trying to raise her spirits. Craig, with a choice of two luxurious dog beds, lay upside down on the doormat fast asleep. When the post dropped through the letterbox on to his chest as usual, he flew round the house in terror. His owner told him he had about as much sense as an earwig that had failed all its earwigging exams.

Her computer monitor was alight and her writing desk had a familiar carrier bag standing on it. She had been poring for ages over reviews and interviews in which her elusive subject had talked about playing Richard III at the National Theatre.

The role had had a profound effect on the actor. In one unguarded moment he said that it was '*like a shadow creeping up on my identity*': another character trying to use him as a host. This was why he had started drinking. And apart from being a barking sot, he was apparently violent. And a coke head as well. Nailing this guy to a chair was going to be easy, like swimming round the world and then wrestling two sabre tooth tigers.

Stence had turned her swivel chair round and had her back to the screen. Her voice could be heard on the phone for miles around, saying the features editor of the *Sunday News* was a shit and the internationally famous actor Declan Mahoney was another shit.

'Lisle I *told* you, I was there twice, he wasn't there twice. *No I'm not!* What do you expect me to do, break into his hotel room at dead of night? *No!* I'm not doing it. I'll google up his cuttings, I'll do the background research, I'll do a down-the-line interview and dot some quotes in before First Night. That's the best I can offer. Or you suggest something. Inspire me, fire me, do what you like. Oh right. That's my fault as well is it?' She laughed miserably. 'OK then Lisle. No, I'm fine. Just half asleep. See ya.'

Stence had worked for Mayhew for seven years. She knew he would keep the pressure up till he got what he wanted out of her. She knew that he regarded her as the best interviewer on his payroll. She had guts and she went deep. She didn't write what were derisively known in the trade as 'come again articles' that buttered up her celebrity subjects so they wanted to see her on a regular basis. She was also the only person on his entire staff who could openly call Lisle Mayhew a shit, which he certainly was.

Craig on the other hand was a greyhound, greyhounds whine and Craig was whining. His slightly cross-eyed gaze had been fixed on Stence for an hour and the dog was asking *why? why? why?* were his desires not met, with monotonous intensity. She would have to take him out before dusk as she wanted to work through the night on Mahoney's case.

She never let the dog down as she had rescued him from a cruel fate. Thousands of ex-racers like him were shot in the head each year for failing to win, their narrow bodies dumped, burned or buried in a landfill site by a man with a mechanical digger, their extraordinary beauty and affection tossed away like so much garbage.

Craig's long, graceful form bounded and bounced as she attached his lead, locked the front door and took him over the meadows where he could race round in figure eights while she listened to the skylarks. One was making its constant call on the wing as it rose dramatically into space, singing both on the inhale and exhale like a set of bagpipes, thrilling itself and anyone who cared to listen. Stence looked up to see it reach the apex of its flying song and then soar down in triumph towards its nest on the ground.

That was when she heard the scream. It was a prolonged high screech of agony and it was coming from Craig.

She raced to the boundary and found him standing in the deep shadow of a twisted tree so that she could hardly see him. A low wire fence had caught his back leg, which was hanging lifelessly, skewed at a strange angle. He had seen a rabbit in the next field and hit the barbs at 40 miles an hour, tangling himself and wrenching his leg free in desperation and terror. Stence nearly fainted.

She summoned the local vet on her mobile and tried to remain calm while four of them carried the dog on a blanket to the van. He was sedated and operated on that evening. The compound fracture was a mess and he wouldn't be going anywhere for a while.

Stence paid the bill, thanked them all profusely and went home to an empty cottage. There she closed the curtains, closed the door, sat by her browsing computer and cried like a child.

She sat there for maybe an hour, two hours, trying to compose her thoughts. She had to work: she had no income other than by writing and vet bills were formidable. It was at times like this, when she was all alone, that a sacred river of inspiration called *Alph* sometimes came to her aid. She hoped he would tonight. Writing was what she did, not just for her living but for her life.

She would sit at the computer for hours at a time, going along the lines from left to right, following the words in their passage across the screen's bright white pages, jumping over them like stepping stones in a fast flowing stream spangled with light. Often she went nowhere because she was trying to impose her will on the magic. But if she did not push, and if she happened to be in a state of grace, that kind of selfless awareness without ego or side or axe to grind, *Alph* would lead them on a dance.

She took great joy in being a part of this magic, swept up in a song on the wing. The words were off on their tremendous adventure and Stence never knew where they would take her. The process used powerful emotions to fuse together thoughts and turn them into words.

'The poet's mind is in fact a receptacle for seizing and storing up numberless feelings, phrases, images, which remain there until all the particles which can unite to form a new compound are present together', thought T.S. Eliot. He said it was 'the intensity of the artistic process, the pressure, so to speak, under which the fusion takes place, that counts.'

And the literary hero she worshipped, Samuel Taylor Coleridge, had told her how the poet 'diffuses a tone and spirit of unity that blends and (as it were) fuses, each into each, by that synthetic and magical power.' It was Coleridge who had christened this power The Imagination. He was the world's leading authority on it, having devoted his life to studying the creative process. Stence, a literary midget by comparison, nevertheless found herself hurtling towards a barbed wire fence:

She was racing to the wire
had heard the cry pierce
sped with more than her speed
to find the broken dog

The short lines on the page signalled that the words coming through were not the same as mere prose words from the left hemisphere of the brain: that they carried a special cryptic intensity and were being summoned from the deep of consciousness where all the fragments fused together in the heat of emotion:

to find the broken dog

Stence covered her face. The feelings were still too harrowing, the connections too raw. She couldn't do it. She had wanted to write

standing in twisted shade
that broke across his back

because it was so strange that she had found the animal standing up, rather than lying prostrate. But instead she wrote

whose shade is that

and could not delete the phrase as wrong. It was then that the new, selfless poem began to compose itself. What rose up from the deep had nothing to do with Craig, or Stence, at all.

Whose shade is that?

She watched as the lines revealed themselves, recalling the Inuit notion that inside every bone is one shape, the artist carving to find it:

Whose shade is that?
Why, it is his. It's his.
It crept up to my feet the other day,
A disembodied voice, a disembowelled past,
The calling card of someone fairly vast
(Though we were introduced in sleep
Like lovers hearing one another snore)
And suddenly a full-blown shadow broke
Across my bow, and he has caught me now,
And will not let me act him any more.

This was about Mahoney's Richard III. But who exactly was this other self? He was not harmless or funny, like the little Tramp who looked back at Charlie Chaplin from the mirror in the prop room, the day the actor had found the walking cane and those shambling trousers and put them on. *This* strange spirit that came to Mahoney was evidently dangerous and rancorous.

The Irishman had found himself under a malign influence, hitting the bottle as Stence's dog had hit the fence. The experience unsettled him. The character in his body began to have views of its own.

For fiendship he outranks Beelzebub
And makes my world a sink.
I flatly answered no
To his great yells for sex and drink.

Why then allow the character such licence? Perhaps because the actor's pride was at stake. They were grand together: it was a symbiosis. The spirit took shape in the spaces between the actor's own thoughts.

But yet he stirs my pride
And in my interim
He sits with his stone stare
And monumental gimlet-eyed despair
Knowing me in the biblical sense
And that I cannot buck his cap and bells.
My bunchback'd toad, my every inch a king:
O who am I that for my sake
My lord should take frail flesh and sing?

Of course! Mahoney *loved* Richard. That was the key to his performance, perhaps all his performances.

Shakespeare's Richard was an evil sociopath, yet this actor had viewed the world through his eyes and forgiven him. He had *sym*pathised with him. He had felt *com*passion for him – these Greek-rooted words were about feeling *with*. Mahoney had not allowed himself to hold his Richard III at arms length in front of the audience as other actors had done, to signal disapproval of the killer king's behaviour. No, the Irishman had publicly embraced him. It was a triumph of selflessness, on a par with being a writer.

Perhaps, thought Stence, she and Mahoney were actually not that dissimilar after all. Suddenly the Irish actor made sense.

He became not a shit, nor a drunk, nor a dopehead; nor a selfish conceited freak who failed to keep his appointments and showed her up in front of her boss and the acting fraternity.

That night, in Spence's study, Declan Mahoney became that highest of all things. He became empathic. A *Bard.*

Chapter Five

The Theatre Royal, Drury Lane was closed to the public for rehearsals. With the sort of sponsorship it was getting from Burns Inc, it could afford the luxury of bumless seats for a couple of weeks.

Behind the main bar, sleeping off a binge, lay Declan Mahoney. Faint but disturbing noises from his slumbers would fail to rattle others in their own cups, wrapped up in their own egos. On top of the bar stood a silver salver, and on top of that a bottle of champagne in an ice bucket and two glasses.

Though Harvey Burns had come into theatre sponsorship under the banner of his beef products, sponsors' fags were everywhere prominent: indeed, you couldn't move for cigars, cigarillos, cigarettes and cigarinos (pink cigarettes for the new young woman smoker). When told about the UK smoking ban, Harvey had said: 'Oh kiss my ass. They don't have to light 'em.'

Dan Loxley was leaning forward in his chair making animated shop talk with the play's benefactor. Obese in his blue pastel suit and stetson and with his eyes bottomless pools, Harvey Burns II could have been mistaken for Orson Wells just after the studio had buggered up his *Magnificent Ambersons*. They had just seen another SSR (or sponsor's special rehearsal). It had stunk.

Dan was getting slap happy. He had not slept well at all, and was overcompensating on the brotherly love, banging Harvey's back with synthetic enthusiasm.

Despite being a brilliant academic and an expert on theatre lore and superstition, Loxley had little insight into what made people tick. If they didn't tick, he simply shook them. He was once misquoted by a reporter as saying that actors were enlarged children but he never denied it. He had had a spectacular breakdown in New York from a mixture of success and researching the occult, but he blamed his illness on actors getting out of parental control. They had apparently given him a hiatus hernia as well, so it was understandable: Dan was simply getting a few things off his chest.

'So she says: "My mother's got cancer of the lymphatic system" – pregnant pause, you know. As if it's my fault her mother is about to turn her toes up in Cheadle Hume to coincide with us turning our toes up in London.' He picked up the silver tray, placed it on their table and began twisting out the cork. 'So I said –'

'This is Ophelia.'

Dan nodded. 'Julia. So I said, Why the blazes didn't you tell me – I'm supposed to be *in loco parentis* aren't I?' He handed his guest a drink, holding the fluted glass by its rim. 'I said It's no good confiding in Padgett –'

'Horatio.'

Dan nodded again. 'I said John's got no more idea than a one-legged man at an arse-kicking contest about his own bloody part, let alone yours.'

As Dan continued with his self-aggrandisement, the top of a bleach blond head and a pair of enormous staring eyes appeared over the bar. The eyes turned unnervingly from side to side, then the head disappeared from view. Dan was still banging on.

'I said, The audience will give you the benefit of the doubt, Julia. They like Ophelia.' He poured himself a drink. 'Even if she is covered in acne.'

'Acne?' The shock made Harvey remove his hat.

'Oh she's got one or two blotches you could see if you held her up to a bare bulb. The trouble with her, like so many of them these days Harvey, is that they think they can model their way through Shakespeare. Christ, they talk about face fascism and wanting to be judged on their abilities the same as men, and then they come to work with one obsession after another about their faces, their backsides, their boobs. Our Sal's the same: Silicone Sally.'

Harvey winced at his cousin's theatre nickname but there was no stopping a man on song.

'I said - ' (and here Daniel burst out laughing from lack of sleep) 'I said, Sal, you're wasting your time with these implants, I said. By the time you're 38 you'll be 54!'

'Sally's a fine girl, Daniel. What should concern you at this point in time is that soused son-of-a-bitch you chose for our leading man. I said we wanted an American in there.'

He produced a virtual tea-chest of cigars, offering the box and a light, and Dan wiped his hand on his jacket and carefully selected one of the dried sausages.

'Oh come on, Harvey – he did play a blinder in *Tamburlaine*. They went for that.'

'Well we have to go with the goddam guy now, right. But he's a liability. I don't want him rat-assed and roaring round my show like one of my ranch longhorns at a fancy tea – and I mean my bulls, not my cigarettes!'

The hero of their conversation suddenly popped his head over the bar, followed by his pet prop 'Esmeralda', a gigantic metal spider. Oblivious, Dan continued, puffing.

'He won't be drunk, Harv. He never drinks while he's working.'

'Well he had better shape up or haul his ass, Daniel.'

'Ah!' exclaimed Dan, suddenly catching sight of his star.

'Aaagh!' shouted Declan in retaliation.

'*AAAGHHH!!!*' yelled Harvey, unnerved by a horrible head and a giant tarantula.

Mahoney stood up. He was small and compact like a prize fighter, and he had the presence of a man who could punch people without touching them. It was an attribute often remarked upon that when Declan spoke, he kept his head still like a stalking lion and then moved unpredictably.

'Did you get it?' Dan asked the Irishman vaunting the bar like a goblin.

'Get what?'

'The money from the telly job so we can buy Harvey a shirt Friday week.' The sponsor's fuse was fairly long but this lit it.

'No call to joke about it! It's your ass Daniel. This ain't one of your British butterball productions.' Loxley offered Declan one of Harvey's cigars. The actor took it, sniffed it, broke it in half and held the pieces on his head like horns. Then he threw them over his shoulders, pulled out a chair and cosied up next to the sponsor whilst addressing his remarks to Dan.

'I believe our distinguished director knows about the threat to his rear end, don't you Dan? Been dreaming of Bosworth Field, so I'm told. Has to sleep with a rubber sheet and a night light, don't you Dan?'

You've sobered up then, Mr Mahoney.' Declan cocked his ear. The three syllables always irritated him. Dan stood corrected.

'*Mahney.* Pronounces it Mahney, Harv, watch that. Te-tiddly diddly, Declan Mahney, bit of the blarney. Back to earth then, Declan, well done.'

The Irishman was pouring the bottle of champagne into a pint mug, slopping it over the sides.

'I've got an idea. You know I told you about Kean following the Ghost out backwards with his sword drawn on the others to protect the Ghost?'

'Edmund Kean?' put in Harvey, always worried about new people in on the production. Declan ignored the interruption. 'Because Kemble had drawn his sword along the ground –'

Dan jumped out of his seat.

'Oh Christ almighty not Kean again Declan! The bloody man belongs to the romantic nineteenth century, son! You can't base a modern performance of Hamlet on bloody Kean!' (Declan was glaring balefully.) 'Haven't I got enough trouble without you running a private – excuse me Harvey – fucking showing of Kean's greatest stage business in the middle of my fucking production – Harvey's fucking production, sorry Harvey. Why not play the Castle scene like I *explained* and we finally *agreed* so I can sleep nights?'

Declan sat motionless, his biceps tensed as though about to fling himself at his foe, his piercing eyes fixed carefully on the drink in front of him. He spoke calmly.

'Kean was the greatest tragedian who ever lived. You are the most microscopic director who ever lived. To implanted women.' He toasted Harvey, grinning in his face.

The sponsor had put up with a good deal but a line had been crossed. Watched by the others he now stormed out and, after a short pause, stormed back in again and retook his seat. The folds of his face shook.

'I warned you. Didn't I warn you about his goddam ego, Daniel? Didn't I say that? I said he'd hurt us with that goddam ego. You wouldn't manage his head-shape, I said that.' Declan was amused.

'It's the opposite of egotism, actually,' he said. 'Of course actors don't have to drink. James gets off on music. Peter O'Toole used to curl up in a foetus position in the dressing room with eye patches on. Anything to sink yourself in the part and avoid your ego floating up to the surface like a dead body all the time. Richard Burton once blurted out in an interview, "Half the satisfaction of being an actor is getting away from your own disgusting self".' Declan's Burton impression was of course very good.

'He also said that he must have been drunk when he said that,' interjected Dan, vexed.

'I thought you were a believer. I understood you to say, in a polished moment, that actors are supposed to be mystics, hosts for the spirit, all that. Or was that just director rhetoric? He's a great rabble-rouser, Harvey, if you've noticed. Pins us to the wall like Cecil B. de Mille. "*Goddam actors! Why are these ten still alive? I thought I ordered a flood scene!*"'

'That's enough, Declan. You're over-wrought.'

'I'm underwrought.'

'Look, Dec lovely – I'm not hoping for miracles. I'm hoping to get you lot and Harvey's money from one end of this play to the other end on Opening Night without the Press chucking their I-pads across the apron. And I'll die a happy fellow. You're right. This play gives me nightmares. Literally.'

'At least you're stoical, *Harv*', Declan goaded.

'I think it's the strength of mind that comes from absolute despair,' observed Dan.

'Oh like Milton's Satan. Never less than archangel ruined, eh *Harv*?'

At which the sponsor finally exploded.

'I don't know how I let you and Sally talk me into this, Daniel! I stand to lose my goddam shirt! And all you can do is sit there talking horseshit about Edmund Kean and Richard Burton – at least they could act! *"We'll get Mahoney. Deal-break casting."* I said you were backing a bum steer with that floosie – what's her name?'

'Julia,' Dan muttered, his shoulders hunched.

'*Julia* having a nervous breakdown over her domestic problems at my expense, and as for you, my friend (his cigar pointed at Declan): I've seen better Hamlets than you so far off Broadway they couldn't see the lights! I've seen better Hamlets than you in the parking lot outside Woolco picking up wastepaper with a pointed stick!'

'Hamlets – they're the little brown ones that go up in smoke, aren't they, *Harv*?'

'Your *ass* is about to go up in smoke,' hissed Burns. The big man got up and this time reached for his stetson. '*And* yours, Mister British Director, sir. Up in smoke.'

'Look Harvey', Dan soothed, 'it's not as bad as all that. They know their lines, bless them. It's just a question of putting the patina on it. Finishing touches.'

'*Finishing touches my ass!*' roared Harvey from the doorway.

''Finishing touches his ass!' mocked Declan, patting his backside. 'Or starting touches.' Giggling to himself, he had another thought.

'*Come back Harv! We need more smoke! They can still see us! Harv? Harv!*'

'Shut up Declan,' said Dan.

'Shut up Declan,' mimicked Declan. He patted the director on the head. 'You know what Peter Brook says, don't you Dan?' His reference to the great theatre guru pulled Loxley's stricken eyes up from the table.

'No. What does Peter Brook say, at this late stage?'

'There's only one thing as effective as a really good director, and that's a really rotten one. His very lack of direction drives the actors to despair and they come across with the performance of their young lives.'

'Shut up Declan.' The Irishman got up and fetched his metal spider, propping it in front of Loxley's nose.

'And keep your props to yourself, you Gaelic git.'

Chapter Six

The Drury Lane appointment was for deep dusk, 8.30pm, highly inconvenient for someone commuting from the bloody countryside, but Stence was on the dot. She had worked herself into a nervous state and wore two deodorants and a dress. Her regular sporty style was abandoned with the exception of two elasticated wristbands which she always wore.

She had brought the carrier bag containing the theatre mascot, intending to give it to Declan as an icebreaker.

'It's you,' sniffed the woman in the theatre booking hall.

Stence thought of a smart response but she showed her press pass for the umpteenth time and resigned herself to another long wait. The receptionist took the plasticized card and disappeared without explanation. Perhaps she was reporting Stence to security again.

The writer nosed round in reporter mode and located the woman's office, putting her head inside the open door. Nobody home, but on the wall next to the computer a large poster of Mahoney as Tamburlaine, a collàge of good luck emails – and a rack of keys. Lisle would want her to do it...

Footsteps. Stence ducked immediately out of the inner sanctum and sauntered in the corridor.

'Mr Mahoney is apparently not expected tonight,' announced the receptionist, holding out the press pass between her thumb and forefinger like a piece of filth. Her all-hours job evidently made her curt with 'dead heads' - the old theatre expression for non-paying bums on seats, such as critics and hacks, though she did add grudgingly: 'Perhaps you can come back in the morning?'

Stence left her theatre mascot at the desk, scribbling a brief message and saying it was for her 'good friend' Julia Lord.

She felt the force of gravity weigh down heavily as her Roman sandals descended those same damn steps. The pall of failure enveloped her brain like a dose of narcotic. This *bloody* bastard of a *sodding* man...

Then a shadow hit her. She stopped short. Her mouth opened and her eyes, glistening with at least one tear, rose towards the figure in front of her.

It was Himself.

Not made out of wax, not a poster image, not beetling dark, nor bog-hopping and swarthy as she had anticipated, but bleach-blond and tanned with the most piercing azure eyes she had ever seen. She had also been wrong about his height, but then actors often looked taller on screen.

'I'm always late, *if at all,*' he said in that familiar voice that dripped masculinity on female admirers. 'Shall we?'

Stence felt as though she had been involved in a collision of the senses. It was like meeting Hitler or waking up in the middle of a surgical procedure: clever though she was, she was out of her depth. Flushing hot like a teenager, she followed the star back into the theatre where he took his key and led her through the building towards his dressing room. Mahoney didn't smile, or make small talk. He put her in a chair, dumped his stuff, and sat down: the Real Thing in jeans.

'I thought you'd be more Irish.'

The words were out of Stence's mouth before she could edit them. She almost gave him her press pass but, thinking fast, switched it to a business card with her contact details.

'Bless you for seeing me at last. I was beginning to think I was making it all up. The *Sunday News* want to find out why you don't like journalists.' She shook her head. 'I'm a writer. I just want to find out.'

Mahoney got up soundlessly and fetched a bottle and tumblers. He poured two glasses of Irish whisky and resumed his seat, sitting with his legs round the back of the chair.

'Who said I don't like journalists?'

'You shut some hack's fingers in your car door. Or window. Anyway.'

'That wasn't because he was a journalist. It was because he had a pea for a brain.' Stence noticed that he said 'brayen'. *You can bleach your hair*, she thought, *but you can't hide your roots*.

'Mr Mahoney,' said Stence carefully, 'I'm not a regular reporter and I don't want you to tell me anything about your private life; only your work. What I want to know is, Did Richard III eat you?'

The famous actor had been asked most things, but registered surprise. Stence bore the blue gaze and continued.

'Lawrence Olivier said the great parts are like cannibals and they eat you. Did Dick the Shit eat you?' Declan gave a slight laugh.

'And that's not about my private life?'

'No, it's about doing your job.' Stence blew up at her fringe, but she had mastered herself now, and was on the case, a fellow-pro.

Declan raised his eyebrows. 'And what do you suppose that is?'

'Identifying with the character.' She noticed that this man was asking a lot of questions and not giving out a lot of information. She would have to get behind his guard.

'I read about the shadow creeping up on you. I know what happened to Vivien Leigh when she played Blanche DeBois. Actors take work home. They learn the words and then they find the character who utters them is more than the sum of its parts. Don't they.' *Get in there,* she thought.

Mahoney suddenly got up and took the glass out of her hand. He nodded towards the door. Stence's heart skipped with shock. He couldn't be serious.

'I'm only trying –'

'Off you go. Tell your editor not to send you here again.'

Stunned and humiliated, she got up and gathered her belongings and her self-esteem off the floor, accepting, by her silence and failure to take back the initiative, total defeat. She had misread the exchanges like an amateur and moved far too early. Interviewers get just one chance and she had blown it. She should have started with small talk like everybody else. But as she left, she looked over her shoulder:

'You loved Richard', she said. 'In my eyes that makes you a bard.'

***

The Loxleys' period cottage master bedroom was done out in New England chintz, the bed covered in a patchwork quilt of red, white and blue patterned fabrics, each diamond stitched with devotion. The lampshades and the low silk padded bedhead, positioned under the only window, were in matching hues marrying Britain and America - Mrs Daniel Loxley had obviously gone to a lot of trouble.

Against the opposite wall was an ornate dressing table and large silver gilt mirror, an antique from her mother's home in the Bronx that was said to be over fifty years old.

Snorting gently in the doubly patriotic bed lay Sally Loxley, wearing black eye-shades. Her errant husband was about to turn in after a late night boozing session with Declan. As he crawled into bed, weary and drunk, Dan burped painfully and rubbed his mid-chest, reaching for the bottle of antacid on the bedside table that his wife had so thoughtfully placed there with a white plastic spoon.

Removing his spectacles Dan swigged from the bottle, turned out the bedside light and lay down to snore.

Without warning a ferocious rattling, as of casement windows, was heard coming from the wall behind the dressing table. This was followed by a shuffling and whistling, accompanied by a loud intake of breath.

Dan sat up, rubbed his face and put on his glasses. The room was illuminated by an eerie light. Where his gaze rested on the dressing table wall there appeared a mysterious window, its casements clattering.

Unable to ascertain whether he was sleeping or waking, Dan shook his head, looked round, slid his feet out of bed and went over to have a closer look.

Suddenly, as he got within a few feet of the phantom window, a face appeared, pressing its nose against the spectral glass. It was Edmund Kean, in full regalia, his eyes desperate and dangerous. He was peering towards the bed.

'Sally,' said Dan, *soto voce*. 'Sally for Chrissakes look at this. Sal.'

'Mmmnnn?'

'Do you see this?'

'Now honey,' purred Sally from her pillow, 'you know I gotta get my beauty sleep or I'll look like Baby Jane Hudson.'

'Sally will you look at this for Chrissakes?'

'Now you're disturbing me Danno, now,' she yawned. 'What is it honey? Is it your oats again?'

Dan edged back to his bedside table and flung his bottle of medicine at the apparition.

'YEAGGHHH!!'

Sally sat up in bed, turning on her lamp and turning her black eye-shades up like swing-wing sunglasses. As she did so, Kean disappeared and the room returned to normal. Except that her husband had smashed her priceless antique dressing mirror.

'Aw my *GAHD* – what the *hell* is going on here, Danno?'

'That! *That!* Did you see it?' Dan was pointing to the now bare wall.

'Did I see what? Did I see what, Danno?'

'Kean! Edmund Kean, as I stand here. It was him!' Dan's red eyes protruded like billiard balls. 'Sally as I live and breath.'

'Danno – would you look at that mess in my bedroom? Honey you are *drunk!* Coming home at (she grabbed her bedside clock) – 4 o'clock in the morning and trashing my things! Why, what did you do, scare yourself in the mirror or something?'

'It was *KEAN! THERE!!!*'

'What? Danno whatever is the matter with you lately? I told you not to go drinking with that damn Declan – that goddam guy will make you crazy like he is!'

She got out of bed and into her negligée gown.

'I told you, whenever you go out with that dipso you see things moving around the room.'

Then, looking in the remains of her dressing mirror:

'Oh my *GAHD*, would you look at that? That crooked Harley Street bastard did it again. I got so many crow's feet I look like my eyes are gonna take a walk. I'll clear up this mess in the morning. I'll get you a Selzer.'

'I don't need a Selzer!'

'All right, all right already.'

'Woman, I saw something – don't you understand? A window, with the – what do you call – the casements rattling, and this *face*, this face, peering in. I was wide awake. Wide awake.'

'Poor little Danno. We gotta get you to a doctor. All those hours you put in. I blame the other actors.'

She took off her gown and got back into bed, saddened. 'Why can't they do the blocking like you've shown them with the cut-outs, like I do? You must have done my little Gertrude bedroom scene fifty times that I know about on account of those retards. You wouldn't be having this trouble with that little Kenny Bran-ner or Ben Cumberbatch or any of those guys – they're *professionals*. They know how to work with a director.'

Dan sat slumped on the edge of his bed as she massaged his back. 'Giving you nightmares. It's giving *me* nightmares. There you are, little Danno. That's it, come back to bed now, honey. It's a bad dream, that's all. Like the one you had last night. And the night before that.' (She yawned, turned off her beside light and replaced her eye-shades.) 'And the night before that. You were asleep.' (She lay down.) 'You dreamt you were awake. That's all it was. You dreamt you saw a window and you got out of bed. That's all it was.'

Dan removed his glasses and cradled them, his hands still trembling.

'Sally, something's happening – I don't know what it is, but it's something to do with this play. I keep dreaming about it. Some augury, I don't know – something in that theatre. I stayed there deliberately tonight, sitting there on the stage with the cardboard cut-outs, waiting. Waiting for something to break, but nothing did.'

'Wrong. My mirror did.'

'Until Declan took me drinking. Am I going mad again, like that time in New York? What is "mad" in this context? I'm too neurotic to be psychotic. It gives you a sort of immunity, doesn't it? At least I hope it does. No, this is not like New York. This is not *psychological.* This is metaphysical, ontological. Is there a direct link between past and present, like there is in mythology? Could something get across that wire? Or is it shadows on the brain, reflections is some inner mirror? I don't know. I've got a bad feeling, that's all, about this play. A very bad feeling about this play. Sal. Sal?'

'*Zzzzzzzzz.*'

Chapter Seven

The lift doors gave out onto the *Sunday News* features department and unleashed Stencie Smith, walking faster than usual, her pupils fixed and dilated. She slung her briefcase on her desk and marched in the direction of Lisle Mayhew's glass panelled room. In her left fist she clutched a piece of paper that might possibly be an email.

Mayhew was on the phone and she wasn't allowed to walk into the editor's office without prior notification. Walking into the editor's office without prior notification, she slapped the paper on his desk and folded her arms, waiting for an explanation.

'I'll have to get back to you on that one, old man. No, it'll be on me this time, OK? Right, no worries. Cheers.' He eyeballed the intruder.

'Stence - what a pleasant surprise.'

'Lisle, you bloody creep. What's all this about sending Fay McCutcheon to do the Mahoney interview? I've been down there *three times* after him and I've done all the background. You can't take me off this now.'

'Sit down, Stencie.'

'I don't want to sit down, Lisle.'

'Sit down. We need to talk.'

Stence sat, sighing angrily.

'Look, I know you really wanted to do this one, but we're on our deadline, and you told me he's not responding. Fay is a movie specialist and she knows Dan Loxley. She may be able to winkle something out of him.' He watched her beadily. 'Sorry about your dog. How old was he?'

Stence looked at her knees, which began to swim. Through clenched teeth she spoke carefully.

'Fay will not get Mahoney to talk. Fay doesn't know his work like I do. *Seven*. He never came –' Stence mastered herself. 'He never came round from the anaesthetic.'

'Well what I suggest is that you go home and have a good cry, and we'll maybe see about a piece next week on the new two-hander at the Aldwych with Alan Rickman. *He*'s a good baddie as well, you'll enjoy that.'

'I'm doing the Mahoney interview.'

'I'm afraid not.'

'Why not?'

'You failed to file.'

'*Fuck you*, Lisle. You want to give my job to Barbie Doll, fine. Tell you what: she can write *all* my copy from now on as well, how's that?'

She got out of her chair and, reaching for his hot coffee, shot it across the desk. There was a delayed loud bang and Mayhew's computer crackled slowly into death. The features editor got up and was bellowing as only feature editors could bellow, though Stence didn't hear any of it. She was already shutting the lift doors behind her. Her only regret was that she'd missed his head with the mug.

***

The Drury Lane stage was strewn with boards and ropes. One rope in particular dangled conspicuously from the centre of the gridiron and imperceptibly waved back and forth with a breath from the wings or a life of its own. Rehearsals were underway again, but even with First Night approaching at deadly speed the actors could hardly be said to have cracked it. This was chiefly due to the presence of desperate Daniel, who had already interfered with this scene more than enough.

Scattered around the stage were the cast's belongings and clutter, including a small antique bear, a gift from an admirer which Julia had taken to her heart and christened 'Fardels'. She had been inspired by Hamlet's famous line: '*O who would fardels bear, to grunt and sweat under a weary life?*' and said that the little mascot would surely bring them luck. Padgett was appalled.

On stage and in makeshift costumes were James, Julia, assorted supernumeries as attendants, and Declan Mahoney wearing his Polonius-killing sword from a previous scene. James Mayne Young was proclaiming in his robes.

'*Where is Polonius?*'

Mahoney in response spoke Hamlet's lines with a peculiar dead-eyed expression, seeming not to be part of the play at all.

'*In heaven; send thither to see: if your messenger find him not there, seek him 'i the other place yourself. But indeed, if you find him not within this month, you shall nose him as you go up the stairs in the lobby.*'

'*Go seek him there*,' said the King to his attendants.

'*He will stay till you come*,' Declan's powerful voice boomed after them. Then the actors looked at Dan, expecting the worst. After a hiatus as big as his hernia, Dan made a noise with his tongue:

'*Tst tst tst tst tst tst*. Hmmmmn. Yes right. We're still wooden, gentlemen. Right, on, on, on, on, Declan's "*How all occasions do inform against me*" we've done, solus, yes, scene five, the Castle. Hmmmn. James!'

'Sir', said the King incongruously.

'Yes, I'm worried about your reaction to the distracted Ophelia you know. Still worried. What was it we decided? Where's Gertrude?' He called affectionately: 'Gert! Sally? Where's my wife, anybody know?'

'She says she has zitts,' Julia explained.

'She what?'

'She says she has spots and has gone to the drugstore.'

'There is no answer to that. Right, I'll read Gertrude. We'll take it from "Enter King", OK? So, Gert: *"Alas look here my Lord."*'

Julia's throat closed like a blocked teapot spout as she attempted to sing:

> *'Larded with sweet flowers*
> *Which bewept to the grave did go*
> *With true love showers.'*

James greeted her: '*How do you, pretty lady?*' At which Dan butted in:

'How do you, pretty lady?' Slow it right down, Claudius, please.'

'How do you, pretty lady?' intoned James. Julia said her next lines as though wound up with a key:

'Well, God 'ild you! They say the owl was a baker's daughter. Lord! We know what we are, but know not what we may be. God be at your table!'

'Conceit - '

Dan snatched off his glasses and stepped between them.

'Ophelia, lovely, you're doing it *again*. You're *playing* at playing the part. You're giving me an impersonation of madness. I want you to do what you do naturally because that's what *comes out* as a result of *your state of mind* – GET ME? Because of what's happened to you, you silly tart, not because I'm standing here telling you to do it, I don't know how many more times. Christ alive! Didn't they do Emotion Memory Exercises at that poxy apology for a drama school you went to? Think about your fucking mum or something. Carry on.'

Julia tore the garland out of her hair and was pacing up and down as James turned on the director.

'For God's sake, Dan – that's a bit thick.'

'Well, I think that's it,' snapped Julia. 'I think I've had it with this. It's understudy time.' James approached her and put his arm round her shoulder but she fended him off and continued pacing. She was now shouting at James.

'What's his problem! Why can't we do the runthrough of Act Four without that *cowson* continually altering direction? We keep switching backwards and forwards going back to the littlest things – you lose your sense of the character and everything. I'm not in a damn film!' she blurted.

'No, the films come later, if we're a good girl,' smoothed Dan, and James was misguidedly putting his hands on her again, whispering, 'Julie. It's OK, Julie.'

Suddenly Declan darted out, turfed James from his path and drew his sword. Julia stepped back, startled. She did not know Declan, but she knew of his reputation for going off like a shed of fireworks.

This time, Mahoney harmed no one. Instead, he placed the hilt of his sword in Julia's hand and stepped sideways, clearing the space between her and the director. As he gestured towards Dan, the others laughed. Declan, however, did not laugh. His blue eyes pierced into Julia as though emitting particle waves. The sword was a prop: it surely wouldn't hurt Dan even if she plunged it into his ribs, though Julia's mind worked mighty hard on the problem.

Finally she slackened her wrist and let the sword point fall to the floor, whereupon Declan took the weapon and sheathed it.

'Greatness in life is going through with your intentions, Julia.' His voice seemed to come from somewhere not entirely human. 'When everybody else takes a step back, you take a step forward.'

He took hold of Julia's shoulders as though about to ravish her with kisses and glared into her face.

'All right? Look at me. Julia. Look at me. You see?' And then he was whispering: '*What though the field be lost? All is not lost...'* the rest of Milton's words muffled from their hearing, disappearing down into Julia's ears.

Dan and the rest of the cast stared at Declan in silence, half amused and half thunderstruck, not sure what to make of this latest Mahoney nonsense. Julia was the only one who moved. She walked over to her little tattered mascot, picked it up from the stage and held it against her stomach, swaying gently back and forth.

At last Dan broke the spell, putting his glasses back on and closing his script with a snap.

'I fail to see what *Paradise Lost* has got to do with it, but still. You might have a point. Fucking fiasco. OK, well, we'll call it a morning, children. But I want you back here at 2.30 sharp. That clear?' And then, kicking a chair out of his way, the director left the stage.

James turned to Julia. 'Julie?'

'Fine, I'm just fine. Would somebody buy me a drink?'

'I'll buy you a drink,' said Declan. 'James?'

'Oh I'm not into these brain-buggering championships, thank you Declan.'

Mahoney grabbed Julia. 'She will, this girl. Are you receiving me?'

'Yes, my Lord.'

'That's the spirit. Where's John of York today?'

'He's gone to the doctor's.'

'Nothing too trivial I hope,' lilted Declan.

'He says our dressing bunker gives him headaches. I don't think it's the dressing room. I think it's John.'

'I'm beginning to get heartily pissed off with our friend here.'

'Who, *me*?' James wondered.

'No, not you. I only hate you, Kingie. Dan. I think he's about to go off the rails without a day return. If he cracks up, I take it we're cancelled.'

'Oh this is typical Loxley,' James chuckled. 'He is worse, though, for some reason, on this play. Something's eating him.'

'A convocation of giant tape worms perhaps,' Declan prompted. And they made for the wings, Julia carrying her 'Fardels' by one arm.

Had circumstances been slightly different, you might have mistaken her for Christopher Robin with a rather different bear.

Chapter Eight

The Sunday after her fracas at the *News*, Stence was standing in Colchester Zoo's underwater viewing tunnel, watching the sea lions turn upside down and torpedo over her head, holding their flippers close to their streamlined souls. Already excellent, they found it necessary to excel even further. Were they trying to impress clumsy, waddling human beings? Surely not: they were closing their eyes. Maybe they had an *Alph* who told them where to swim.

The writer lost herself in animals. Paradise regained away from words, from people, deadlines, egos, conversations fraught with feeling that hit the buffers and the thousands of petty hurts and humiliations that dragged her, with all her insights and poetic flights of fantasy, down to earth.

She was 39, unbeautiful and unemployed. Having no family, she had become utterly dependent on a dog that had suddenly vanished, leaving her his entire estate of two beds and a water dish. Stence was not fashionably helpless. She didn't sit in sorrow on the floor swallowing mood-altering drugs. Instead she puffed her asthma inhaler occasionally and took herself off to commune with nature, just as the alienists used to expect their lunatics to do in the old asylums. She had traipsed the fields near her home, but without seeing many fellow creatures. Here she could at least look them in the eye.

She had moved on to the meerkats when her mobile purred in her pocket.

'Stencie? Hi! Remember Julia - the world's worst Ophelia?' The actress laughed. 'I got your number from Declan.'

'Julia!' Stence's face lit up. 'Hi there - how's the *Hamlet* mob?'

'Oh – heroes in damp socks, you know. First of all I just wanted to thank you for my little bear – he is so *old!* I love him *excessively!* I know you said he was from a theatre but wherever did you *get* him?'

'A strange Celt, actually.'

'You mean there are two of them?'

'I was approached by an Irish guy trying to sell him as a priceless antique. Apparently he came from Tunbridge Wells theatre – the Corn Exchange?'

'Well that would certainly interest Declan,' Julia's voice narrowed. *'Anything* to do with Edmund Kean.'

'Kean performed there, did he?'

Oh yes. And I'm sure Mr M will tell you *all* about it. He's ob– an expert on Kean.'

'Declan won't tell me all about anything, Julie. I'm off the case. He won't speak to me because I tried to ask questions about *his work*.'

This clearly amused the actress, though she was careful what she said. 'Dear me. What did he think you were going to ask him about?'

'Plus I chucked my job up at the *Sunday News* over it as they were sending in their film floosie to do the interview instead of me.'

‘Oh so *that* was it. Only it’s in the paper, Stence – we’re just reading it here. This was really why I rang - you’re famous, dear!’

‘*What?*’

‘It’s in the rival Sunday rag - doesn’t have a picture of you or anything, but it says you, Stencie Smith, *blah blah blah*, freelance journalist, 41, chucked a pot of coffee over the editor. “*Sunday News* features editor Lisle Mayhew, 53, was taken to the Royal Free Hospital suffering from irregular heart rhythms, but was discharged the same day.” It says he is not pressing charges or anything.’

Stence laughed out loud. ‘I don’t know how they got hold of it. Some stupid sod in that features department I guess. I never *touched* him. All that happened was his computer went *phutt*.’

‘Tell you what,’ conspired Julia. ‘You come over here and sit in our dressing bunker and talk to John and James. I’m sure you could do a little piece for *The Stage* or something.’ And then Julia surprised her new friend by going well off record.

‘People need to know what kind of man this Daniel Loxley MBE really is.’

The meerkats sat up high but couldn’t make out where the twolegs with the funny noisebox went.

***

The Loxley lounge had one wall entirely lined with books, and Dan was balancing on the edge of a chair with an arm outstretched to the topmost shelf. Pulling down one book after another and blowing off the dust, he was on a frenzied mission in his lunch hour. He was not helped in his endeavours by Sally, her facial rash covered in Camomile lotion, trying to impress her husband with her mastery of Gertrude.

'"*Hamlet, thou hast thy father much offended*",' whined Sally.

'"*Mother, you have my father much offended*",' recited Dan parrot-fashion, still rifling through his bookcases and flinging various titles about.

'"*Come come, you answer with an idle tongue*." You see? I know Gertrude. I got a bead on her now Danno.'

'"*Go, go, you question with a wicked tongue*."'

'"*Why, how now, Hamlet!*" You see? You see how I do that Danno? You see how you've helped me with that, my own living Will Shakespeare, helping me with my interpretation, and you even look like the guy also. So OK. OK! "*Why, how now, Hamlet!*"'

Dan was beginning to lose more than his book. '*It was here!* I saw it when they were decorating.'

'Well I don't know – you lent a lot of books to that actor who was playing Iago for Michael last year. What's it called again?'

'*Edmund Kean: Fire From Heaven*.'

'And it's by Edmund Kean.'

'By Raymond Fitzsimons.'

Sally searched. 'Is this the one?'

'*Fire from Heaven*, not *Shakespeare's* fucking *Festive Comedies*.'

Sally was shocked. 'Honey, don't swear at me!'

'Well what have you done with it, darling?' Dan appeased. 'It was definitely here, along with all my books on theatre superstitions and the occult. Where the hell are they?'

'I didn't see that one,' Sally smarmed.

'Oh? Which ones *did* you see?'

'I never touched them!'

'Sally! Sally? Come on. I need to look something up for Declan.'

'Oh damn Declan the whole time! That Irish ape the whole time.'

'What's got into you?'

'That guy is bad news for you Dan, and you can't see it! He's undisciplined, he upsets Harvey, he keeps you out till the dawn breaks – and then he knows you have a stomach condition and he pours drink down your throat! "Hiatus hernia" I mean.'

'That's no bloody concern of yours!'

Sally's mouth fell open. 'Not my concern? Not my concern? *I have to pick up the pieces!*'

'Oh Sally shut up!'

Well you're getting worse than you were in New York, Daniel. I didn't want to say it. Than when I first met you.' She paused, brushing the dust from her ample chest. 'And that's why I put those damn black magic books in the garage.'

'Oh Christ!'

'That's why you got sick in the head the last time! Go ahead. They're all in the damn garage! Read 'em all. I can always go back to the Bronx. I got family! I don't have to watch you break yourself apart researching – *hobgoblins*!' She was weeping slightly. 'He's a malign influence, Harvey says so, also. You've never shouted at me before, never. In all the two years of our marriage! I know I'm not as educated as you are, but you said I had other features!' She was now weeping in earnest.

Realizing his tragic flaw, Dan dropped his books and went over to his wife, cuddling and caressing her.

'Oh Sal – come on darling. Sally. I'm not researching the Black Arts: I just want to look something up about Edmund Kean's life, that's all.'

'Well OK, Danno. I'm OK if you're OK. I'll fix you some lunch and then I'll go look for your book. You want pastrami on rye?' Disappearing into the kitchen she called, 'Or shall I do you my egg plant salad? You loved that before. What was it you wanna look up about the little Kean guy?'

'About when he was playing Sir Giles Overreach,' Dan echoed mildly.

'Oh. And what did he do that one time?'

'He was possessed by the Devil.'

Egg plant in hand, Sally leaned round the door.

***

Late that night, their spot rehearsal having ended in the usual chaos, Dan Loxley knelt alone on the stage, trying yet again to sort out the blocking – the actors' positions and moves during their speeches. These are normally marked out on the stage with gaffer tape to show the actors their positions prior to furniture being placed, but Dan still favoured good old fashioned chalk so that he could keep rubbing out. The action of the play depended on the blocking clicking into place: if the director couldn't get this choreography right, there was no structure for the cast to hold on to and they were flying blind.

Dan was surrounded by cardboard cut-outs of his cast, and by the oddments and debris they had left behind - Yorick's skull, its cigarette bent upwards, two empty bottles, a pair of fetid trainers and so on. Leaning against a chair leg was Julia's Fardels Bear, its antique head tilted to one side. Feeling the ill-effects of Declan's potato juice, the actress had carelessly left her mascot behind.

Dan's cardboard figures, which appeared to have been cut out of Shredded Wheat packets, were moved up and down with tremendous care, and then moved back again as he pushed his glasses up his nose.

'*Bastards!*'

He shifted the cut-outs into a line, got up from his knees, then opened a folding chair and sat on it, viewing the blocking from above. Still no good. He shifted them all back, muttering under his breath.

'Polonius: "*A will come straight...*" Hamlet within: "*Mother mother mother.*" Queen: "*I'll warrant you; fear me not! Withdraw; I hear him coming.*" Pit-a-pat. Polonius hides behind the arras. Enter Hamlet. No! Enter Hamlet. No – no good, it's got to be from here. "*Mother mother mother,*" pit-a-pat, be-dom, be-dom. *Tst.*'

Dan clicked his lips, leaned back in his chair, took off his glasses and rubbed his eyes. Then he sighed loudly, put his glasses back on and looked at his watch. He ran his eyes over the goods and chattels on the stage: a haversack, a helmet, a T-shirt, Fardels.

Absently, he picked up the Bear, examined him, and sat the little fellow on his ursine backside. Then he rearranged his cut-outs yet again. Finally he stood up and kicked the cut-outs with considerable feeling, sending them flying round the stage. The exertion caused his glasses to fall on the floor. He picked them up preciously and looked them over.

'Thank Christ for small mercies. I don't know. What are we going to do? What am I going to do? Go out of your mind, Dan, why don't you! Bloody Harvey. Bloody Declan. Bloody bastards.' At last, he gathered up his cut-outs, heaved a final heart-rending sigh, and exited stage left.

It was some moments before the single spot came on of its own accord and picked out the Bear.

Chapter Nine

Outside the theatre, Padgett and Julia arrived in ceremony in John's new old car - an American army surplus jeep *circa* 1963, with its wartime colours and markings still visible in the orange street lighting.

'John – it's awful!' Julia grumbled, jumping down from the running board. 'I think my brain may have come loose. Hasn't the thing *got* any suspension?' James and Declan were already investigating the vehicle's unusual features, such as rusted panels, full canvas winter kit and sticking plaster headlamps.

'Not bad for two and a half grand,' said Padgett, patting the bicycle wheel intended for steering. It's the Hotchkiss M201 – the French rebuilt a lot of them. Bloke was going back to the States yesterday, so I ferociously beat him down.'

Declan seated himself next to Padgett in banger heaven and the pair tore off round the London streets, followed by a cloud of deep blue smoke. They were discussing Julia. By the time they returned, Ms Lord and James were themselves deep in conversation.

For their own protection, they had decided to have Stencie Smith keep a record of the production goings-on prior to Opening Night. They both felt that if things went off the bridge, it was hardly fair that their careers, or John's, should land in the river. Ranks had closed against Loxley, and even Declan was now having serious problems with him.

As the evening rain began to sluice London's lights and Padgett rode off in search of spare parts, Declan took Julia and James to his dressing room.

'I've got some potato juice Padgett brought me back from the Far Country,' he told them. 'If it's what I told him to get, you open the bottle and a genie pops out and grants you three wishes.'

They stood in darkness inside his star doorway.

'All that Satellite TV money and he still can't afford a light bulb,' cracked James, vainly flicking the switch, the low sounds of Handel's *Messiah* rising up from his iPod. Declan, who always removed electric light bulbs in his dressing rooms, lit a candle as his guests looked round.

On one wall they could make out a phone, a worktop and mirror. But commanding all, in an ornate gilded frame, was a copy of the George Clint portrait of tragedian Edmund Kean. He was in costume as Sir Giles Overreach, in which part he had taken London by storm in 1816. Other than that there were four chairs, a bed covered with clutter, a sink, a sofa, a futon mattress rolled up on the floor, and a door to a private annex. Not much for a star of Declan's drawing power.

Beneath Kean's picture sat Yorick's skull on the worktop, another Longhorn cigarette in its mouth. There were also a television, a DVD player and two unopened bottles, one of which Julia immediately recognised as the brew she had once tried to flush down the sink.

'There's enough light in this world,' said Declan with a glint. 'What we need is a little privacy. Bow down, little mummers, for this is your King.' And he held the candle up to the portrait, its eyes seeming to beetle in the dancing light. Julia was fascinated.

'He is gorgeous, Declan.'

For only the second time, Mahoney noticed Julia's gender (the first having been when he put his spell on her in rehearsals). Finding glasses, he poured out the questionable bevy then switched on the DVD player, inserting a disc. The monitor was dusty.

'I want you two to look at something I've been working on for my series – for all these so-called millions I'm supposed to be getting. Only – if we're going to save this production, we need to pool our ideas. Now, have a look at this. Awp!'

He looked round for something to wipe the screen with, and chose Julia's mascot.

'Hey – that's my Fardels Bear!'

'I thought lucky mascots were for James's generation,' said Mahoney, throwing the treasure back at her.

James responded: 'That's right. I believe peacock feathers are unlucky, that saying the tag-lines in rehearsals is unlucky, and that there is a divinity that shapes our ends.' And he turned his backside towards them as he lay down next to his *Messiah*.

On the screen appeared a brown-faced image of Declan in black, against a black background. He was miming. The eyes were strange, the effect achieved using white contacts with black centres. Mahoney's own voice provided the soundtrack, reciting the lines from Hamlet's '*To be or not to be'* speech. The voice spoke abruptly and without sentiment. By the fourth or fifth line, his reading went deliberately out of synch with the image, so that the words were spoken faster than the mouth opened and shut. The face meanwhile grew paler and paler: it slowed and declined until it was white, staring, silent and haunted, with the voiceover continuing remorselessly to the end. Then the recording blanked out, and James and Julia sat bemused, unsure how to respond.

'It separates body from soul,' said Declan in his normal voice. 'Or as my fellow Irish bard Yeats would say, "Things fall apart; the centre cannot hold." Well? What of it? Julia?'

Julia pulled one of her shiny blonde wringlets out of her mouth. 'You're asking me? I think it's fascinating. Love the goggly eyes.'

'James?' Declan really was making an effort with others.

'Bit arty-crafty for Harvey Burns Inc, wouldn't you say?'

'True. Just showing off. We're dead in the water. Plus the white eyeballs would only be seen from the front rows anyway. Pity though. Drink up.'

Julia had already swallowed hers and held out her glass. She looked intently at their peculiar principal.

'Do they expect too much of you, Declan - being the star and all?'

'No. Why?'

'Well it must be more difficult for somebody like you –'

'There is nobody like me,' Mahoney gunned back.

'No, but – I mean, people are paying to see you. They're not paying to see us, are they?'

James rolled over towards them. 'Thanks, Julie, very much.'

Declan looked severe. 'They're paying to see *Hamlet*. I couldn't give a flying fuck whether I come up to their expectations or not.'

'You don't care about that sea of faces, waiting for Mahoney to take them somewhere?'

'No.'

'*No?*'

'I don't consider great acting to be any of their business.'

James sat up and scoffed: 'Caw!' At which Declan sprang from his cross-legged position like a cat and stood next to the portrait, pursuing Julia with a baleful look.

'Would you like those eyes boring into you, Julia? The direct gaze addresses itself to the soul, the identity, doesn't it?' He began to pace. 'If wild animals look into each other's eyes, it usually presages a fight. People suffering from performance anxiety are often affected by the direct gaze. Olivier asked his fellow actors, in his months of agony from stage fright, not to look into his eyes during a performance, did you know that? No. Because to be out there sacrificing your ego to the unknown, naked and vulnerable, is to be able to feel other identities crowding in on you. And the force of the gaze comes from here – the pineal gland. The middle eye. Actors and poets are very vulnerable to it because we're toying with identity.'

The pineal gland,' murmured Julia, hardly recognising her own voice. 'Is that like the evil eye?'

Declan didn't answer, but like a flash produced his metal spider from a cupboard and set it in front of her.

'*Oh God!*' shrieked Julia. 'Esmeralda?' Declan nodded. 'Mascot?' Declan shook his head.

'*I* have a mascot however.' Julia sounded drunk. 'He came from a theatre. Matter of fact he came from the Corn Exchange in the Pantiles, Tunbridge Wells, while it was being refurbished.' She flopped Fardels Bear from side to side and Declan immediately altered the quality of his attention.

'The old theatre building?'

'*Yes.*' *And now I've got you, mister*, Julia thought.

'You're sure it was the old Corn Exchange?'

'*Yes!* Why?' She sounded casual enough.

'Friend of mine performed there on occasion,' Declan said, picking up the antiquity and examining it.

'Oh, *not* our Mr Kean! Really? You like him a lot, don't you.'

'I don't know, he's dead. But a lot of the time he was alive he was dead drunk, so I suppose we'd have seen eye to pineal gland in the Dog and Duck.'

'Why the obsession?'

'It's not an obsession.'

'I'm sorry.'

'Kean was the greatest actor who ever lived,' said Declan simply.

'How can anyone make that assessment if they never saw his performances?' Julia was being deliberately provocative.

'His performances have gone down on record, every detail. There's nothing that's ever been written about Kean that I haven't read. He invented studying for a character, sitting in asylums to study madness - all that. He laid the foundations of modern acting. He brought characters to life.'

'I thought he had syphilis,' Julia chided.

'Oh he was a wencher. He'd have three of them in the dressing room during the interval and say as he closed the door, "Can't do much tonight as my clap is very active."'

'Oh God. Charming person.'

'But he was an ACTOR, Julia. He knew what the barriers were and he knew how to burst through them, because he had more moxie than any of his predecessors. Nothing stood in his way – not friends, family, fame, fitness, vanity, ego – nothing. Put it all in the melting pot, everything he had. And then by making himself a *nothing*, by expunging himself, he could pluck spirits out of the air. Like this. Like a magician. Look at those eyes. George Clint's portrait of him as Sir Giles Overreach. The Drummond portrait of him as Richard III. They're not human eyes.'

'I thought that was artistic licence – you know – Kean! Da-da!'

Declan was now talking to an auditorium inside his head rather than to his fellow-actors. His monologue transformed the number one dressing room into the stage of that very theatre, Drury Lane, circa 1816.

'After *The Beggar's Bush* and the *Merchant of Bruges*, he decided the time had come. *A New Way to Pay Old Debts*, by Philip Massinger, in which Sir Giles Overreach goes mad on stage. This was to be his apotheosis, his becoming a god. He knew exactly the risks; that he would have to give himself to this unmitigated villain and let Overreach shake him about in his teeth, and he knew that he was going to have to communicate the most intense evil, terror, rage. But even he didn't know the sum of it, the cost of it.

'Was he afraid? No. He stood on the still point of the turning world. He paused, and surveyed the theatre, and the audience, and the darkness, and he drew in his breath as though drawing in his pity, because he knew what he was going to do to the theatre, and the audience, and the darkness. And then he held his identity in the palm of his hand, like this, and blew all his fond love to heaven.

'And then it began. His features turned livid. He opened his throat and a scream using him for an instrument rattled him, shook him violently, and reverberated round the theatre, hitting the walls. One by one, women in the audience became hysterical and had to be removed. Lord Byron in his box next to the stage suffered a convulsive fit. Mrs Glover, an experienced actress, had to be helped to a chair, because of the sight and sound of Kean, ripped and convulsed by Overreach's evil, by his negative identity, like a refulgent head, turning and turning on his shoulders. Joseph Munden stood transfixed, his eyes riveted on Kean's face. "My God", he said, "is it possible?"

'And the audience in the pit, who rose to him, could see the cast in Kean's eyes, his wild eyes, as though he were gazing at something here, in front of his forehead. The supreme sacrifice. Which is why they paint him with his eyes boiling into the back row. Possessed. Literally. Greatness.'

Julia had dropped her mascot and was watching Declan with wary admiration.

'And that's what you think acting is.'

'Yes.'

'And you'd like to be possessed like that.'

'Yes.'

'Coo.'

James now turned round, his headphones having fallen round his shoulders.

'Oh for crying out loud. Have you quite finished, Declan?'

'Why, what's the matter with you?'

'Nothing's the matter with *me*.' James gave an ironic laugh.

Declan suddenly began reciting Lady Macbeth's famous invocation speech, summoning the forces of darkness. It was guaranteed to unsettle a superstitious actor like James and Declan glared him in the eye.

'*Come you spirits*

That tend on mortal thoughts:
unsex me here –'

James snapped: 'Declan! You don't quote that in the theatre during another play!' But Declan went on with renewed emphasis:

'*And fill me from the crown to the toe top full*
Of direst cruelty; make thick my blood,
Stop up the access and passage of remorse –'

James stood up, yelling at the top of his voice. 'Declan! *DECLAN! Stop this! Declan!*'

As Mahoney continued the unspeakable speech, James became increasingly agitated, pulling at the man's arm, and his shouting formed the background to the dreadful invocation.

'...*That no compunctious visitings of nature*
Shake my fell purpose, nor keep peace between
The effect and it! Come to my woman's breasts
And take my milk for gall, you murdering ministers,
Wherever in your sightless substances
You wait on nature's mischief! Come thick night,
And pall thee in the dunnest smoke of hell,
That my keen knife see not the wound it makes,
Nor heaven peep through the blanket of the dark
To cry, "Hold, hold!"'

James roared: '*NO!!! NO!!!* That's a *rotten* and a *wrong* thing to do in a theatre! God! Bless this theatre! Bless these four walls and everyone in them!' He took his iPod and aimed it like a Tazer at Declan, turning up the volume of his *Messiah* as loud as it would go.

Julia, who had remained calm throughout, finally stepped in.

'James! James, turn it down, please! Please. Goodness me. Thank you, James. My eardrums.'

James was still incandescent. 'That was unacceptable, Declan, in a theatre where we're doing another play.'

'All right, James,' Julia soothed. ''He's egging you on - look at him. I do think you're a bit ghoulish myself, Declan, by the way. Something working away in there, I don't know what it is.'

Declan's ribs were tickled. He gave a manic laugh, followed by a spluttering noise, as James looked at him steadily.

'He was quoting Milton's Satan in rehearsals. What is it, Declan – some sort of affectation? Or are you just very literary today?'

'I'm literary every day,' Declan shot back. 'I'm Irish – we invented it.'

'Would you invoke the Celtic gods?' Julia was smiling.

'Yes,' said Declan quietly. 'I'd sell my soul to the Devil for the definitive Lear, the best Hamlet. There's nothing I value in this world more than to lose myself and gain that. To be larger than life. To be timeless, for the instant of that performance. To be a god.'

'You don't think the risks are rather staggering,' Julia said through gritted teeth.

'No, I don't.' At which James interjected:

'Congratulations, Declan – I'd say you're heading for the Richard III ward at Tavistock Loony Luvvies' clinic, personally.'

'Shut your mouth!' snapped Declan, disappearing into his annex. James looked at his feet.

'I'm beginning to think I'm the only sane person in this whole set-up. Oh, John – he's sane, he comes from Yorkshire, sorry. There's you on the brink, there's Daniel hanging well over the edge, there's Declan of the Devil's party – how can we fail? Now can this particular production of Shakespeare's *Hamlet* conceivably come to a bad end?' He burst out laughing. 'You fancy him, don't you?'

'Ssshh!'

'Strumpet! Hath she forgot already that brave prince, Padgett her lord, not three hours absent from the dressing room?'

'*Ssshh!* Shut up James. I'm not a stage door Jenny.'

'Creatures of the night, eh? A lot of women have this fixation about evil men. Why is that? Why holdest thou this brief for evil men? Or these briefs? *John, John, John, the grey goose is gone, and the fox runs away from the town-O.*' Julia picked up her belongings and confided:

'John doesn't know me.'

'He lives with you.'

'He lectures me, like Dan. He makes me –'

Declan returned, grabbed Yorick's skull and stuffed it up the back of his shirt.

'Right, then,' he announced, misshaping himself like Quasimodo. 'By your leave, kind sir. Shall we away to see the four-eyed Führer?' He bowed extravagantly at James, affecting a thick Irish brogue. 'All right, Mayne Young? Give me your pardon, sir, I have done you wrong, but pardon't as you are a gentleman. This presence knows' (indicating Julia) 'and you must needs have heard, how I am punish'd with a sore distraction.'

'You're bloody mad, Mahoney,' laughed James. 'As a hatter.'

Declan extinguished his candle, and the three of them left the room to Kean's portrait, its insane eyes still glimmering in the darkness.

Chapter Ten

Next morning, Stence was looking out through the window of Julia Lord's bijou garden apartment in Chiswick, holding the actress's Persian cat. Julia's mother let her want for nothing, at least that money could buy. Out on the driveway, John Padgett's legs protruded from underneath his Jeep. The sounds of metal being hammered and expletives being hurled were audible from the couple's minimalist living room, with its bleached pine furniture and Lalique crystal tastefully lit in small alcoves.

Julia came in from the kitchen with tall glasses of iced coffee and a copy of *The Stage*. Her blonde tresses were casually swept up in a knot, revealing two faint love bites on her neck.

'There was something in here about how Hollywood directors famously used to bully their stars – here it is: "Tyrants Behind the Big Screen." You can borrow this, Stencie, so long as I can have it back. John and I may need it to look for work after 27th April.' She was quite serious.

'But would modern actors actually put up with this?' Stence frowned as she tried to hold the paper with the cat standing on her lap.

'Oh believe me, we do. It's a market force – remember the vast majority of actors are usually unemployed. They are at the mercy of anyone willing to give them a job.' Julia sat with her legs curled round on the cream leather sofa. 'Of course not all directors are like that. But if you are unlucky and get a despot, he can make life pretty grim.'

'And Dan Loxley is one of these shoguns.'

'I have to be careful what I say, Stence. But we need help, really. Off the record – and this is all off the record so far as John and I are concerned – it's affecting the whole cast.'

'No worries Julia. I will never quote anybody unless they ask me to – you have my word. In fact –' She tore a sheet from her notepad, scrawled a brief statement and signed it. 'There you go: that's a confidentiality commitment from me before we start. I told you: most of my work is ghosting. I don't get books by selling people down the Swannie. There is one slight problem, though.'

The door of the lounge flung open and Padgett stood in the frame. He looked like the victim of an oil slick.

'That *fucking* thing.'

'Iced coffee, darling? Remember Stencie Smith? She's a *journalist*.'

'I know who she is. Hallo again – can't shake hands. I've just put a new exhaust on it – now the bastard sump's leaking.' He disappeared into the kitchen to ruin the sink enamel. Julia looked at Stencie, glanced heavenwards and mouthed: '£2,500', pointing downwards with her thumb.

'You were saying there might be a problem?' she asked.

'Well, Declan won't want me in the theatre. He gave me the order of the Irish boot.'

Julia looked round at John, who had just returned, rubbing his hands with Swarfega.

'Disguise her,' he said bluntly, and wandered out.

Chapter Eleven

Morning rehearsals were underway. They were tackling the Castle scene and the set was practically being built round them. The simplistic Harvey Burns plan to throw vast dollar power at the famous theatre and 'just hold it dark' for three weeks while the cast rehearsed everything *in situ* was being shown up as a disastrous folly. They should have used rehearsal rooms like everybody else.

Loxley's prevarication meant that the schedule was already convulsed like a cut snake, and the technical rehearsals and set cues had been thwarted and put back by further runthroughs to get the actors 'off book' and confident away from their scripts. Sawing and banging could be heard in the background as scenery carpenters fought with time, and the actors were tense and irritated. They still had the frustrating technical rehearsal to look forward to, with lighting rigging going in and sound cues and prompts being tweaked, before proper dress rehearsals could get underway with their long-awaited costumes.

They knew they were late for the last train and they knew Hellboy had their tickets.

The rope previously seen dangling from the gridiron was still hanging down but had been incorporated into the set with a flagpole on the guard platform.

The atmosphere was stress-managed. Loxley had ceased to prowl, and stood with one foot on a folding chair. Unfortunately, although this was supposed to be an uninterrupted runthrough of part of the play, he still couldn't help making little niggling changes. Declan, not required for this scene, sat with his knees round the back of a chair, keeping abreast of the many alterations.

On stage were John as Horatio, a 'Bernardo', a 'Marcellus' and Tim Godsthorpe, a jobbing actor in his 40s who never quite lived up to his potential because of his shyness, wearing studded boots and playing the Ghost.

In the stalls sat Julia Lord with her mascot Fardels Bear and her new stress counsellor Dr Fay Raymond, whose platinum bob and tinted glasses concealed a magnificent lack of knowledge about cognitive behavioural therapy. Julia had asked that Dr Raymond be allowed to accompany her during the build-up to First Night, as a precaution against her having to leave the production on health grounds. The management team had had to concede they might be risk-exposed in this instance.

On stage, 'Bernardo', in full armour, was clattering back and forth in front of the wardrobe mistress complaining of chafing when Loxley clapped his hands and whistled the cast into position.

'Right – from: "*Peace, break thee off*". Go.'

'*Peace, break thee off! Look where it comes again!*' stage-whispered 'Marcellus'.

'*In the same figure like the King that's dead!*' replied 'Bernardo', bending his knees and rubbing his inner thighs.

'*Thou art a scholar; speak to it Horatio*,' said 'Marcellus'.

'*Looks it not like the King? Mark it Horatio*,' Bernardo hollered, as Padgett stepped up to his mark.

'*Most like it harrows me with fear*,' droned the Yorkshireman as though reading cricket scores.

Dan sprang into action.

'John – sorry – can we have you downstage just a smigeon more so we can see you address your mates without taking your eyes off him? Ghost, you're making a bloody racket.'

'It's the rake,' mumbled Tim Godsthorpe.

'Do what, Ghost? The rake? It's not the rake, it's you. Can you tread on the balls of your feet more? Oh dear. Now, I don't want anybody touching you, either, which reminds me – Hamlet!'

'Hallo.' Declan's voice pierced the gloom.

'Er, when we ran through Act One five at "*Haste me to know't*" and I said to touch your father?'

'Yup,' sighed Declan.

'No, it won't go. It makes the Ghost tangible, and it'll put the audience off. It's not worth it. No, don't touch him, Dec.'

'You suggested it. I said it was a fulsome gesture for a recluse.'

'Yes I *know* I suggested it, but right now I'm *un*-suggesting it. I don't want the ghost touched, right? Remember you had your own way on pre-recording voiceovers for all your asides and soliloquies so you didn't have to do stage whispers or natter to the audience. Give me a break here. Right. Yes, what is it, you dead git?'

Tim Godsthorpe was as tall and lean as a street light but with less electricity. 'Sorry, Dan,' he mumbled, 'but I've got a slight problem.'

'What's up with you?' Dan sniped.

'I still don't like putting my finger up in the air when I hear the cock crow.'

'And why is that?'

'It makes me look a bit daft,' Tim murmured. 'Can't I just exit at "*Tis here*"?'

'Then the audience doesn't make the connection.'

'Well, they're not simple,' Tim mumbled. 'I don't have to go' (and he cupped his hand to his ear) 'Hark, hark, the dogs do bark!' Several of the actors laughed. Dan looked wounded.

'Get out of my hair, Tim.'

'OK then?'

'Yes, yes, we'll see. Would that make you happy?'

Tim was surprised to be asked such a question, which made his voice even more inaudible than before.

'I don't know about *happy* in this play.' Dan put down his prompt book. His tone was sarcastic with hydrochloric acid as a chaser.

'Oh I see - it's the lack of *felicity* that's the problem, is it, rather than just the finger. Well, let's have it. Come on. Let's have the alarm and despondency out here where I can see it.'

Utterly miserable to have been singled out, Tim spoke in a monotone with his chin on his chest.

'Well, perhaps I shouldn't say this, Dan, and I can't speak for the others, but my confidence is at an all-time low. I thought I could act till I started this play.'

'Well if you *act fast*, you might be able to get down to the Job Centre and cut your losses, mightn't you, hmm? Godsthorpe? You silly sod. You wouldn't be in this production if you couldn't act. None of you would. You are here because of your marketable talent. Some day when you're a star like that Irish ponce over there, I shall expect you to support me when I'm a broken down old director.'

'Bit late for that,' murmered Tim, 'in my case, anyway.'

'*Do what*?' Dan's own larynx worked extremely well. 'Marlon Brando was a great mumbler, you know. Did you know that, eh? In 1946 he was auditioning for a part in Maxwell Anderson's *Truckline Cafe*, and the director, the great Harold Clurman, couldn't hear the lines. This was the up-and-coming young Brando – nobody had ever heard of him. And Clurman couldn't catch the lines, but somehow his instincts told him Brando should get this part. Read poorly, mumbled for days, head sunk on his chest as if he were trying to keep the script a secret, like this, *mumble, mumble*. Do you know this story? Anyway, this went on and on – author's agent wanted the part re-cast, but Clurman said no – he could see that *behind* this veil, this membrane, was a talent waiting to burst out, like the Alien out of the eggcase. But this young man was like you. He was scared. Director couldn't boost his ego – tried everything. Nope. Wouldn't or couldn't open up. So one day, Clurman asks everybody else to leave, and then he turns to Brando, and he says, "I want you to *shout* your lines." So, Brando raises his voice. "Louder," says Clurman, "louder!" And by now Brando is looking across at him a bit dangerously, you know? Anyway he raises his voice again. "No, I want it LOUDER," says Clurman. "Climb the rope!" – and he points to a rope hanging down from the gridiron above the stage. So, Brando looks up and he begins to climb, and Clurman says, "Now, keep shouting your lines! Go On!" So up he goes, up, up, up. And the rest of the cast have come out of the woodwork, and they see Brando up there and think he's gone apeshit. And as he comes down, he's got one or two little veins standing out of his forehead and they think he's definitely going to pop Clurman one. But he doesn't. "Right," says Clurman quietly, "now I want you to run the scene normally." And Brando recovers his composure. Speaks up, no problem. Clear as a bell. No more mumbles or fear of divulging himself. And in a few days he was playing that scene like his autobiography. Opening Night and *every* night afterwards, his performance got one of the most thunderous ovations Clurman had ever heard for an actor in the theatre. True story. That was a mumbler. Right? I'll give *you* "Hark, hark, the dogs do bark." Any questions? Look at this shower – look at you. Cast of bloody castaways.'

Declan was actually smiling.

'For a split second, there, Daniel, you looked like old Will Shakespeare.'

'That was me, pre-incarnated,' replied Dan. 'I'm English, you see. He wasn't a bloody bog-hopper, our Will.' And the director broke into a mock jig. 'He wasn't a bloody clog-dancer, was he?' Dan jigged about.

Suddenly Declan, not to be challenged on anything Irish, got up from his chair and began to hardshoe round the stage with his hands on his hips, the rest of the actors clapping to the tattoo. The end of the dance fetched loud cheers and applause, Julia standing up in her seat and waving her arms back and forth extravagantly. To Stence's horror, this brought Declan over to the stalls.

The blue eyes pried into Julia. 'When Kean first started, they made him dance Harlequin. They thought that was all he was good for,' said the actor, leaning across the seat.

'I knew there'd be a connection,' answered Julia, literally fluttering her eyelashes. 'Declan, I'd like you to meet Dr Raymond – she's my stress therapist.'

Stence's brain lit up like a bulb: *you snake in the grass*.

'How ever do you do? I've never actually touched a shrink before,' said the Irishman, proffering his hand with utter charm. Stence felt her skull on fire in the damn wig. She shook the slender fingers firmly and turned towards the stage as if mesmerised by Dan Loxley, who was speaking. She knew Declan would instantly recognise her voice even if he didn't see through the makeover. He was an actor, for God's sake – they take everything in, like an MRI scanner. True, it was a fairly professional job and Julia had secretly involved her own makeup girl and all the cunning arts of the prop room. Also true, Declan had eyes like a boa constrictor. Stence would have to hope that he wasn't paying much attention to her during that abortive ten-line interview.

'Everything else OK?' called Dan. 'That makes a change. All back here at 2 sharp. What are those you've got on your feet, Tim?'

'Trainers finally legged it out of the theatre on their own,' enunciated Tim quite clearly.

'Oh, only I've got a pair of flippers you could have worn,' Dan replied, climbing down from the stage. 'Hamlet – can I have a word, mate?'

The men disappeared and Stence's lungs went back into action. It reminded her of her near-fatal asthmatic childhood. She followed Julia out, wondering a) whether she could still do her student party piece South African accent after all these years, and b) how to murder Julia and make it look like an accident.

Meanwhile the stage had emptied apart from 'Bernardo', who stayed behind privately hitching his crotch.

As he bent down to grab his helmet he spotted Julia's Fardels sitting in the front stalls, and being the decent fellow he was, picked up the airhead's precious mascot to return it to her dressing room.

Chapter Twelve

The master bedroom had suffered. Sally Loxley's dressing mirror had had some running repairs but would never be quite the same, and there was still a sorry stain on the wall where Dan's bottle of hiatus hernia medicine had exploded. The bed was immaculate, adorned with a new duck-egg blue satin duvet cover and six enormous red and white damask cushions stacked in front of the headboard, the way Sally had observed in *Hallo* magazine. But some things can never be put right by beauty alone.

It was lunchtime, and Dan was standing with a glass of Aqua Libra in one had and a large house plan in the other. His leading man was sitting on the dressing table, filling a chunky glass with Jameson's whisky. Their chilli cheeseburgers could be savoured from some distance away.

'About *here*,' Dan was saying as he placed the flat of his hand high up on the wall stain and Declan curled his lip. 'And then I was over here – this way.'

'What did you do, throw up over it?' Declan jibed.

'And now look at this,' enthused Dan, pointing to a spot on the house plan. 'When it was built, *this* was the front of the house. See? Covered in pargeting, with one window – here. And then they rebuilt the facade to face away from that development - I talked to the agents.'

'*Is it haunted?*' exclaimed Declan in a panto dame's voice.

'Oh Dec, don't take the – '

Sally came in, flinging the door open. She surveyed the scene furiously, but said not a word. Instead she marched angrily over to the marital bed, straightened the satin cover and brushed and banged each cushion in turn. Then she looked round and slammed out.

'I'm not taking the piss,' said the actor. 'Couple of racing trainers I knew stayed at an inn in Tewkesbury. Playing cards in the evening, one of them puts his hand up to his ear because he feels something on his face, and his ear's bleeding. That was the first thing. So by bedtime, this one has the wind up, but oddly enough he sleeps like a baby. The *other* chap wakes up in his room with a start in the middle of the night, thinking he's felt somebody touch his leg and hoping it's the receptionist, and when he opens his eyes he sees a window on the wall across the room – rather like this – idea.'

'Didn't see Edmund Kean, did he?' Dan's spirits were sinking.

'Sadly. But he asked at the desk in the morning if anybody else had had trouble with that room, and suddenly a can of furniture polish went *zzzt!* like this,' said Declan, demonstrating with a tortoiseshell hairbrush.

The door burst open again, and Sally strode across the room with two coasters and a dishcloth. She wiped furiously at a mark on the dressing table, slapped down the coasters, picked up her hairbrush, glowered at Dan and stormed back out.

'That's nice' hissed Dan, trying to keep his voice down but getting animated. 'I'm talking about – this was a bloody *face* looking in. Looking like this – *at the bed!* I thought my number was up!'

'Fancied Sally,' said Declan, tactlessly loud.

'*Ssshh!* And we're on the first floor here!'

'Perhaps he had a ladder.'

Sally re-entered with a bottle of hiatus hernia medicine and a spoon. She banged these down beside her husband and slammed out.

Dan called after her: '*It's Aqua Libra for f-fishwife's sake!*' Then he sprang up and ran out of the room. There was some loud shouting, with the words '*giving you nightmares*' and '*hobgoblins*' clearly audible, after which Dan returned, looking cowed.

'We can't bear to hear about – ' he whispered, gesturing with his head towards the wall.

'Drink?' Declan smirked. Dan put his hand over the top of his glass to signal no. 'Go on. Chaser? Hobgoblin?'

'*Ssshhh!!!*'

'I'm not saying I disbelieve you, Daniel. But I've had dreams that were so vivid I've woken up and found myself out of bed with my hand on the light switch trying to have a look. Plus you're a touch hyped up here.' He paused. 'Did Sally see it?'

'Oh drop dead, Mahoney.'

Dan turned his back and tried to refold his house plan, getting into difficulties. Declan clambered on the bed in his shoes and stood behind him trying to help. Managing to rip half of the document away, the Irishman was overcome with mirth.

'Give it here a minute!' he spluttered, folding the tatters.

'And get off the bed, Dec, for fuck sake! She'll have conniptions! *Get off!*' Declan jumped down and went back to his whisky. Thoughtfully he filled Dan's empty glass as well.

'All you need is a proper drink!' Declan's voice rang out without any propriety: 'I'm not saying there's no supernatural – you're preaching to the converted, Daniel. It would be unnatural to conceive of a universe *without* a supernature! But we are in the middle of a little old play –'

'It's got nothing to do with the play – can we keep it down a bit, Dec?'

' – about a little old *ghost*,' continued Declan as loud as before, 'and by the laws of association, the shaping spirit of imagination, hhmmm?' And moving Sally's cushions out of the way, he sprawled on the bed for a lie-down.

'Don't you think I've considered all that, Dec, *for Chrissake*?' wailed Dan. 'I have done a *bit* of research on the occult and theatre superstitions, haven't I - and will you get off there, Dec, what's the matter with you? Half my books in the – garage – are given over to the damn subject! *God alive!* If anybody's entitled to be dismissive, it's me, if what I'm telling you were not authentic. And *I* think this is straight out of James I's *Daemonologie*. You want to know what I think? *That's what I think!* Shakespeare was up to his *balls* in it!'

The door opened once more and Sally came through it with a Dyson cleaner. She plugged it in and began whirring the crumbs off the carpet. Dan reacted.

'Oh just leave it, darling, for sod's sake leave it!' He pulled out the plug.

'Don't you speak to me like a shop girl, Daniel. I'll do what I damnwell please in my own goddam home. And just what the hell do you think *you're* doing, stenching the bedroom out with food and pouring that poison into your face so you wake me up every night seeing hobgoblins – '

'It's Aqua Libra!'

' – and talking about Edmund Kean and Satan's nostrils to impress this Coke head – *the oldest Hamlet since Mel Gibson* – '

'Olivier was 40 in the film,' Dan weighed in wretchedly.

' – and where this one comes from, they still talk to *LEPRECHAUNS*. Am I right? You just slob around all day on other people's *beds* drinking from stills and figuring out how to raise Cain with *LEPRECHAUNS* – isn't that how they do it in *CORK?*'

'Cork?' whooped Declan, close to splitting his sides: 'Cork! I was born in Surrey, madam. How do you think I got past the English Directocracy? '

'Oh well, Mr *MA-HO-NEY* from *SURREY*, my husband has a hiatus hernia! And when you pour *ALCOHOL* into him and screw up his subconscious talking about *HOBGOBLINS*, he gets sick. And when he gets sick, I get mad. And when I get mad, everybody watches my lips, because I don't need a ouija board to raise Cain or a stage to stick pigs – I can do it in *REALITY!*'

'Sally!' pleaded Dan, 'Sal!'

Sally took her Dyson cleaner and, thrusting the nozzle attachment in the direction of Declan's crotch, stormed out. Dan looked at Declan, shrugged, smiled, toasted his friend and took a gulp from his glass. As the whisky hit his tonsils he spluttered and had a choking fit.

'Aaaw! Is that from the Buggers' Brewery? No wonder you fall into comas after rehearsals.' Dan blew his nose. 'From Surrey, old man?'

'Yup.'

'I thought you were Irish Irish.' Dan put his hand over his face, as downstairs the sound of the front door being slammed off its hinges signalled Sally's departure.

'My father was Irish,' Declan announced. 'My mother's from Box Hill.' The door slam having robbed him of any diplomatic skills he may have possessed, Dan laughed:

'Good lord! We'll have to keep this from Hollywood and even Bollywood. Bad for the old charisma.'

'Why?' snapped Declan, bridling.

'Well, not exactly Edmund Kean's catchment area is it, *Box Hill*?'

'What's that supposed to mean?'

'Just what I said.'

'Kean lived in Richmond and died in Richmond. That's Surrey, by the way, not Virginia. Leased a little theatre there by all accounts.' Declan was squeezing a sachet of tomato ketchup over his chilliburger. 'But then you knew that, of course. You're the world's expert on Kean's catchment area now, aren't you.'

'No, I thought you were his spiritual godson.'

Declan looked up and his blue eyes shot sparks.

'I know your game, foxy Loxy. That's why you brought me up here, isn't it – so you could tee me off like you did with Tim Godsthorpe, feeding me a bit of the old Kean legend? Eh? Get a performance out of him yet? Eh? Look at me. You stage-managed this, didn't you!'

'Oh - ha, ha, ha,' mocked Dan humourlessly.

''S'blood, do you think I am easier to be played on than a pipe?"

'Ha, ha, ha.'

'That little Director's speech about Clurman. Liked that. Mmnn. That was good. But do you know *why* actors can't get off the ground when they can't get off the ground?'

'No idea,' said Dan, carefully tidying up the ruined bedroom.

'Well, I'll tell you. It's because of you. It's because of the Director. You know what happens in Clurman's Hollywood? The actors all limp round in a circle waiting for the Great Man to tell them what they feel about their characters. That's the American disease. Then there's the British disease – because we're even *more* self-conscious over here. Actor manager – he's dead and rotten. We're all *ensemble* players now. We've all got our eye on the *baton*.' The actor began moving his head up and down as he delivered his diatribe.

'Nobody can afford to get out of his depth, or go stark staring mad like Kean would have done; no, we're all listening to the pitch, watching the little light on the end of the baton, and we can see who owns and runs and shapes the British theatre, and we know it isn't us because we're all watching the little light, watching the baton, wondering am I getting carried away with the bourgeois individuality of this character like Brecht said I shouldn't? What did the Director say at this point? What inflexion did he want for this? *SELF-CONSCIOUS*. Grounded! Feet glued to the planet Ego by this force of gravity. And then mission control, in the person of our eminent Director, comes along and says, "Right, you can get up, now, a bit. You can get above yourself, now, a bit. I *want* you to get above yourself! I want you to get up there!" He likes to think he inspires, he invokes. He *doesn't*. He makes the average actor defend himself. That's why they've *got* their chins on their chests in the first place! Why they mumble. Why they need a rope. It's because of you.' Declan was sitting down, looking into the bottom of his Jameson's. 'Because of you.'

'I agree with you,' said Dan with solemn conviction.

'What? You haven't sniffed it.'

'No, I agree with you. This is the age of the great director, not the great actor. With respect. It's our turn now, mate. You're looking up our noses now. Conversely, failures are largely our failures.'

'*With respect?*'

'What?'

'You said, "*with respect*".'

'Yes, I respect your abilities. I don't think you've cracked Hamlet – perhaps he's a bit too intellectual and equivocating for you – but I respect your abilities. I think you've probably got more plain courage than most actors of your generation. That's why I asked for you.'

'But you think I'm about to go down the drain in this.'

'I didn't say that, at all. Theatre's a funny business. Anything can happen. Olivier thought he was going to be *rubbish* as Dick the Shit until he turned to face the audience on opening night and got a bolt of lightning. Just do me a favour and stay off the sherbet for five minutes. You're a very remarkable young-*ish* man. I think you can still pull it off.'

'You do?'

'I do.'

'You think I might yet buck the British Establishment on this one?'

'Your performance is your performance. I might prod you a bit,' Dan smiled.

Declan suddenly reacted by flinging the remains of his food and tomato ketchup across the bed, followed by his drink. He looked at Dan savagely, evidently hoping for a fist fight.

'Yes, well,' Dan said quietly. 'This is why actors are commonly regarded as children; why you're known as the Neurotic Profession and the Luvvies; why the administration don't trust any of you because you're all up and down like a fiddler's elbow. You asked me what I thought and I told you.'

'Right.'

'And you feel a lot better now.'

'Right.'

'Say something, then, even if it's only a stream of Celtic obscenities.'

Declan's lips were tight. Fixing Dan with a prolonged baleful glare, he got up, knocked his bottle over and left.

Dan sat musing on the bed, and then spoke softly to himself.

'And as the Irishman said, as he watched all his belongings roll down the hill in a wheelbarrow, "*I cannot do justice to this situation*."'

***

Back at the theatre, a domestic from the agency was singing quietly while she cleaned the mirrors in Julia and John's empty dressing room. She tidied up the makeup trays and stood the good luck cards neatly on the worktop. Then she hung Julia's head garland over a chair and placed Fardels where the actress could see him. The mascot now wore a luggage label like Paddington's, saying 'This Bear belongs to Julia Lord.'

As the cleaner propped him against the mirror she noticed something funny about the Bear's little eyes. She picked him up and looked more closely, frowned and set him down again. Finally she snatched up her bucket and broom, opened the door and briskly rubbed her hand on her overalls.

Chapter Thirteen

It was 4 a.m., humid for late April and the sheets clung like film to fast food. Stence lay on her side looking at an empty dog bed. She couldn't quite get her brain round the idea that she would never see Craig again. She *must* see him again: he was her family.

She felt that events had somehow been jolted out of their proper course, and that reality must surely return to normal if she slept and woke and slept and woke enough times. Yet precious reality seemed to have been permanently injured, and by something that took just seconds to occur. Maybe reality would never go back in shape, or heal over. Maybe abnormal was the new normal, and if it were, it had sure put paid to her modest dreams.

Lately she had also lost her ability to fantasise, which used to keep her company when the small hours were bare. Through the voile curtains the dark was thinning and she could make out one or two shrub shapes in the garden. The first lonely bird was singing to itself, saying it had survived another night. She got up and went into her study with a bottle of mineral water. If only she had been a smoker.

She turned on the computer and her mechanical servant lit its screen for her. It worked all hours – it was a mean gig for an appliance. She entered her password and checked her emails: not a plink. No word, no work.

She would have to carry on with the theatre assignment after all, though it was becoming deeply humiliating. The *Stage* hadn't even commissioned her, and said they would wait and see what she could come up with. Loxley was an extremely high-ranking director with good libel protection. It didn't necessarily safeguard either the writer or the publication that any allegations were in quotes, or true. Such articles were always hazardous. Could she find a national newspaper to take the story, one with a larger legal battery?

Stence's brain was running round the dog track. She felt foolish masquerading as a therapist, and couldn't believe she had let Julia and Padgett talk her into it. But she still desperately wanted to get Declan Mahoney to talk to her. It was not just a matter of work any more, or ideas that burned hard in her head. He made the pores of her skin open.

She looked at the Google search bar and typed in 'Edmund Kean'. The trawl was rich.

She discovered the glittering little man had rocked London audiences as Richard III and Shylock in 1814, after theatre impresarios had initially wiped their boots on him: he was considered too short and insignificant for Shakespeare's heroes. It had been a bitter Christmas for Kean, and not just because the Thames froze over. While the diminutive actor danced attendance on theatre bosses begging for mercy over a contract problem and longing to work, his young family nearly starved and his son Howard, whom he adored, died of disease and hardship. Kean told his wife Mary: 'If I should succeed now, I shall go mad.'

After he had mesmerised London with his performances, the tragedian never forgot and he never forgave: it was said that he could detect a sneer across Salisbury Plain. But his power as an actor was unlike anything the capital, or indeed the world, had seen. Stence's great hero Samuel Taylor Coleridge said it was like watching Shakespeare by flashes of lightning, and the critic Hazlitt wrote: '*He bore on his brow the mark of the fire from heaven*'.

So *that* was the source of that haunting phrase. So *this* was the man who inspired Declan Mahoney.

Stence suddenly sat back in her chair. She had the distinct feeling that she was not alone in the room. She looked round. Bereaved dog-owners sometimes pick up traces of their lost pets: fleeting sounds and sights to comfort their grief. Nothing there, of course: wanting does not make it so.

She switched off the computer, got up and looked at herself in the bathroom mirror. Walking about with Julia Lord had daunted whatever prettiness she might have had, but she had to refurbish herself in a hurry. Today was 23rd April. It was Shakespeare's birthday and Harvey Burns Inc, may they rot in hell, were throwing a damn party.

***

The theatre Green Room was similar to Julia and John's dressing bunker, but with a few more tables and chairs. In place of the dressing-room worktops there was a counter for serving light refreshments and a coffee machine.

Dirty dishes and mugs were piled high in the sink and the bins were full. It was a bad time for their charlady to be off sick with Opening Night just around the corner, but the actors were willing to make do. Burns Inc had after all hired a catering firm for the evening and elaborate party preparations were underway at London's Bronzegrove Hotel in Belgravia, with its lavish banqueting hall and its famous rooftop garden - a cigarette magnate's lofty refuge.

At this very moment, flower garlands were being twined and webbed around the long dining room's red marble columns; glass candlestick displays and ice carvings resembling crystal skulls were set to adorn the tables. To top it all, Hamlet himself would be making a guest appearance in the person of Declan Mahoney. Amid much pomp, he would be seen cutting a cake in the shape of Shakespeare's head, and the press were coming in force.

In sad contrast at the back of the theatre, John Padgett was alone among the dirty dishes and in costume as Horatio, with the unusual addition of cricket pads and a bat. On a portable radio shaped like a bluebottle's face he was listening to the cricket and practising forward defensive strokes, the hallmark of the Yorkshire game. He simulated each delivery with a narrow whistling sound, and signalled the ball hitting the bat with a clocking noise of his tongue.

The cricket was a displacement activity. John's Jeep had blown up fairly spectacularly on Chancery Lane and he had had some difficulty getting the breakdown service to come out as he was not a lone single woman. Plus none of the breakers yards he had rung up so far had Jeep parts of the required vintage.

When all else failed, John usually took to sport, as he did on this occasion. He was fed up with the whole production and he was not interested in face-saving sponsors' parties either. All he wanted was a pint of Tetley's bitter and there was none here. As a matter of fact there was none of anything here, apart from Julia's Fardels Bear, presiding over their ruin.

'*Wssssss........ddqqq. Wssssss.......ddqqq.* And it's the googly – yes! *Wssssss.....ddqqq.* Straight as a bloody arrow.'

Unnoticed by John, something funny was going on over on the counter. As an eerie light briefly flickered into life, Fardels flinched slightly, and suddenly his eyes glowed bright red. The two tiny beads shone with such malevolence that had Padgett been aware of them, he might well have been out for a duck.

The light returned to normal as Julia came running in. She was lugging several large store bags and she puffed and panted. Her new writer friend was on an urgent trip to Richmond, she knew not why, and had dropped her back at the theatre in time for dress rehearsals.

'You'd better get into Ophelia quick. Burns has thrown a fit,' warned John, taking his pads off.

'Oh my God oh my God,' said Julia, throwing her garments in a heap. 'Stence was telling me she doesn't see that much harm in Loxley, you know.'

'She *what*?'

'She says he sounds quite inspirational as academic directors go – just a bit of a bully. I was rather annoyed actually!'

'Well she's not seeing him in his true colours, is she,' John groaned.

'Anyway I told her she'll have to make herself up for the party tonight as I shan't have t – '

There was a hubbub outside. The door came ajar and Sally, in costume as Gertrude, peeped in.

'Do you have my Danno in here?' Sally's voice was ready to explode with excitement. 'Only he has just *got* to see this. This'll kill him stone dead. '

Her voluptuous form squeezed through the door and finding no Danno she urged: 'You guys have just *gotta see* this!' And she turned backwards to signal to the others. 'Right – wait wait wait – no put the thing back on – that's it. OK, now ready? Julie, are you ready for this?'

'I'm looking – what am I supposed to be looking at?'

'*OK BERNARDO'*, Sally yelled: '*LET IT RIP!'*

Julia looked startled and the others collapsed in gales of laughter as 'Bernardo' removed his helmet. His hair was standing on end.

***

The tall grey stone Norman chapel of St Mary Magdelene stands in a leafy enclave behind Richmond's high street shops. Stence parked up and wandered into the deserted building, her footsteps echoing after her.

Behind a plastic chair in one back corner she found a white wall-mounted commemorative plaque between drapes, with a man's cameo. The profile was stereotypical and might have represented anybody, but the inscription vouchsafed that this was a memorial to Edmund Kean, erected by his son Charles in 1838.

The year of death was given as1833 at the age of 48, but there was no birth date. However Stence had done her research. According to his passport and other sources the tragedian was actually just 44 when he expired from brandy and syphilis.

In the opposite corner, set in the stone floor beside some infant Sunday School furniture, was a stark black marble slab. Its message was simple:

Beneath this stone lies EDMUND KEAN, actor, died 1833: the sun's bright child.

Stence sat on a bench and a wave of inchoate emotion swept over her. Under her feet lay the man many believed to have been possessed by the Devil on the stage of the Drury Lane Theatre in 1814: an artist who burned himself away in pursuit of his genius.

She was beginning to follow Declan Mahoney on his dangerous journey into this other man's soul, and in her case there was no career imperative for such a risk. She was being drawn into the maelstrom simply because she happened to see the link, because she happened to be a writer, and because her brain happened to be susceptible.

She was following Declan, Declan was following Kean, and Kean was following playwright Philip Massinger into a character who came, like most purely fictional characters, from heaven knows where. That character, invented or intercepted by what we call imagination, had unleashed on London theatregoers forces utterly beyond their comprehension. Those who sacrifice themselves for their art make a perilous quest into the dark depths of human consciousness. And when they do, they often drag others with them.

Stence went home and wrote her own small poetic tribute to this great man. She couldn't give it to the deceased, but perhaps she might give it to his empath.

Chapter Fourteen

The ranks of zoom lenses and cordon of *paparazzi* outside Belgravia's Bronzegrove Hotel that April night gave tourists the powerful impression that Queen Elizabeth II was about to alight from the black limousine on the forecourt. Many of them were milling about among the film and theatre fans, hoping to get a glimpse of Her Majesty, when Queen Gertrude stepped out in all her finery among the throng, lifting her Tudor skirts above the gutter.

Sally Loxley was in her element: she had more chutzpah than Mel Brooks and the flash photography lit her magnificent beaded hair as she shook hands with her cousin Harvey Burns II on the carpeted steps.

She was accompanied by her husband, heralded by Burns' publicists as the director who would 'bring the Bard's true power back to London theatregoers'. The fact that Loxley resembled Shakespeare physically had been a key selling point in all the press releases. Loxley grinned and wound his arm in the air, a cross between a wave and a blessing.

In the next car, Padgett was telling Stence not to overdo the South African accent and James Mayne Young was trying to get his crown straight. His magnificent emerald velvet Claudius robes had only just arrived from wardrobe and he was worried about dragging them in the dirt. He had been asked to refrain from smoking as the tobacco smell was difficult to shift, and he was more nervous than a usurper at an investiture.

The only sunny personality, emitting from the second limo, was Julia Lord, who was more beautiful and regal than many film actresses and graceful as a ballerina. Her midnight blue satin period dress was rouched at the sleeves and pinched at the waist in a low V above swooping skirts and her blonde hair was elaborately braided. She carried a small nosegay of lily-of-the-valley, a present from her ailing mother who was unable to attend the bash.

Inside the sunlit great dining hall, decked from floor to ceiling with crystal and roses, the feast was already underway and spilling out onto the rooftop gardens. Scores of critics and theatre luminaries were seated round the huge U-shaped table arrangement in anticipation of boring speeches and exciting wines, television cameras were angled into every celebrity orifice and Harvey Burns in full evening dress quaffed champagne and spoke at the top of his voice about how Shakespearean culture affected Texas.

Stence found the whole affair a gross confidence trick, half way between a debutants' ball and a farmers' market. It had nothing to do with art, or acting talent. It brought the world of tinkling celebrities and poison pens into the mystical theatre that she loved, where the greatest actors were striving to bring spirits to life.

Through her tinted lenses she was watching Dan Loxley, much maligned by his cast, smiling and quoting the Sonnets. She had no intention of libelling this man. All directors were surely bossy: they had to be. They were the ones who had to body forth the playwright's vision and get the actors' performances to weave into a tapestry empyrean on Opening Night.

Stence was discreetly introduced to the press during dinner as Julia Lord's 'associate' rather than her 'therapist' as they had previously agreed, because Loxley and Burns felt that Julia should not be flaunting her 'stress' before the media during the production. Stence had argued against the change but went unheeded. One or two reporters even took 'associate' to mean 'live-in lesbian lover' and Stence feared unwanted column inches were already knocking out of the fax machines. Padgett was furious; Julia failed to grasp the seriousness of the situation and giggled prettily into her third champagne.

Sally Loxley laughed flirtatiously with a circle of male admirers about the whole fiasco and even lined up the fluted glasses and ran her red polished fingernails round the tops to make a tune. Stence did not drink and was utterly miserable. Wisps of her real hair kept sneaking out from under her wig so that she was constantly disappearing into the marbled ladies' loo to adjust herself.

The night wore on, and by 10 p.m., the fine vintages having been guzzled and Shakespeare having been toasted to charcoal, Burns and Loxley were seething with anxiety. They had given interviews to journalists large and small but there was still no sign of the man himself, Declan Mahoney. The cliché 'Hamlet without the Prince' had spontaneously sprung to several different headline-writers' minds; the ice skulls were melting and the Bard Cake, complete with unlighted birthday candles around his ruff, lay uncut in the centre of the table.

Burns and Loxley feared that their errant star had forgotten the gig and lay in a drunken coma in some nearby tavern. Burns blamed Loxley for this. Dan said that perhaps the actor had met with an accident. In any case they were going to have to make an announcement shortly, as the PR people were twitching their asses.

Just as all hopes were about to fade, the double glass doors suddenly swung open at the end of the hall, and two smiling hostesses in the doorway began a round of applause that steadily rippled round the room and broke out into cheers.

As jaws dropped and eyeballs widened, Declan Mahoney, in full Hamlet regalia and with his Timberwolf Stillbad on a chain leash, strode down the centre of the hall towards the tables, the flash photography one continuous glare.

The actor bowed extravagantly to his crowds, marched up to Dan Loxley and sat on the table. Picking up an entire leg of lamb with his gloved hand he offered it to Stillbad, who threw himself down on the carpet and lay chomping noisily. The animal, its sharp teeth bevelled by a veterinary surgeon, had evidently been inured to unusual events by Declan's busy social schedule. It seemed a lot calmer than Loxley, for example, who grinned for photographers and whispered through clenched teeth:

'Where *the fuck* have you been, mate?'

‘I’ve been up to London to see the Queen,’ Declan replied. ‘Let’s get this over with.’

The caterers had set the centre table with an elaborate floral display surrounding the Bard Cake and a cigar-lighter and carving knife at hand for the candles and the slicing.

Declan ignored the lighter, picked up the kitchen blade, took hold of Loxley’s dinner jacket and held the knife at the director’s throat. Press bulbs popped as the actor smiled and posed before releasing Dan and plunging the knife into Shakespeare’s bakery visage.

Stence laughed out loud. It was a triumph. Later on she was sitting with Julia and Padgett in a corner discussing the 650 different meanings of ‘stress’ when Mahoney and Stillbad shook off their entourage and made their way over to the table. Mahoney and Julia kissed each other on the cheek and exchanged luvvie greetings while Padgett unaccountably sprang up and patted his knees, offering to get the Irishman a drink.

Stence could feel her heart thudding in her chest. She had been practising her South African accent and decided attack was the best form of defence.

‘Did you have Stillbad from a cub?’ she asked.

‘He was orphaned actually – he came from a zoo in Uganda before the animals were used for target practice.’

‘He’s awesomely beautiful. I can’t believe you subject him to this – the only wolves that have survived persecution are the ones that are furtive and avoid human beings.’

'Provided people leave him alone and don't make any stupid moves, he's fine.' Declan glanced at Padgett as the Yorkshireman sat down bearing two manly tankards and nothing for the women.

'He is an *Angst Beisser* isn't he', said Stence, looking at the wolf and then into Declan's steel blue eyes. 'I read your press clippings and I've read Konrad Lorenz. "Tamed" wolves, no matter what you do to train them, will bite from fear.'

'You've read my press clippings?'

'Well, a few of them,' Stence covered herself, nervously blowing up at the fridge of her wig. 'I read that he bit some idiot reporter. Good luck to him, I say.' And then she began talking to Stillbad as though to an old friend.

Declan had spotted the fringe-blowing gesture in a nanosecond and knew who she was, but decided against challenging her as he wanted to see how the scene would play out. He figured the accent would have to give if the wig didn't.

Julia was bubbly and exuded charm, but Stence noticed that every so often Declan broke off their flirtations and turned towards her, examining her disguise.

'So how's the counselling business?' he finally asked. 'Any famous clients on your books?'

'Crying out loud, Mr Mahoney. Patient confidentiality you know.' They both laughed.

'Only I was wondering if you could do anything for me.' Stence was aware that Julia and Padgett's conversation had cut dead and that their eyes were fixed on her lips.

'That would depend on you,' she said, arching her eyebrows. Outwardly calm and professional, she felt as though her heart might be making her eyeballs beat in their sockets. She turned to the wolf and addressed her remarks to the handsomest face in the room, the only one to whom she could really relate. His ears moved and his yellow eyes, perhaps mild, perhaps murderous, focused on her.

'I lost my greyhound the other day, Stillbad. He ran into a barbed wire fence. I miss him, he was a wonderful friend.' A catch in her voice told her to stop.

'The more I see of men, the more I love my Dogfather,' said Declan.

He was now staring at Stence and she felt unequal to the situation. She got up gently and slowly so as not to alarm Stillbad, and smiled at the group.

'It's getting late - I have to go. It was a pleasure to meet you, Mr Mahoney. Goodnight Julia; John. I'll be back at the theatre in the morning.'

'Just a minute,' said Declan, getting out of his chair, 'I think you've got something in your hair.' For an instant Stence thought the game was up, and that he was onto her wig. But he leaned towards her and whispered in her ear – and it was quite unmistakeable –

'*Do you know anything about ventriloquism*?'

Stence didn't miss a beat.

'Oh you mean speaking in tongues.'

And then the writer smiled at Stillbad and left.

Chapter Fifteen

Declan arrived at the theatre next morning earlier than usual. This was not because he was keen to start dress rehearsals or see his voice coach or check on his costumes, but because he had not been to bed.

Outside on the steps a sprinkling of admirers had positioned themselves, holding their digital cameras forward, and a woman fan and her six-year-old son were waiting with a movie still for the actor to autograph. The little lad stepped forward and lisped:

'Can you please' – and he breathed audibly with concentration – 'sign this picture, Mr Moany?'

Declan took the biro out of the child's hand, writing with a flourish and grinning as he handed back a keepsake of the theatre never to be forgotten. The woman looked at it later: it said, '*From one dwarf to another.*'

Julia and John were in their dressing room kitting up, and Julia was trying to reassure James, who was having an anxiety attack and inhaling one of the sponsor's Longhorn cigarettes. They were afraid he would set off any smoke alarms the theatre might possess but thought this the lesser of two evils: they didn't want him barfing in their sink again. Julia patted his back and nipped out to the nearby chemists to buy him herbal calming pills.

'Sorry, old man,' James frowned at John, his *Messiah* going on his iPod.

'On dear no, not this in here as well.' John pulled the iPod out of James's grip and interfered with the volume. 'What do you have to have this on all the time for? Eh?' They sat in silence. James replaced his crown, drawing passionately on his fag.

'Helps.'

'Looks like it.'

'Bit of religious harmony – good for the old tempo-rhythms.'

'Teh. Bloody security blanket. Like this is.' He flicked the St Genesius pendant round the King's neck.

'Nothing elevates you, does it John?'

'No, but then nothing petrifies me either.'

'Oh I *see*,' James put in, looking at Padgett's size elevens. 'Now I understand why your feet never leave the ground.'

'Look, I don't want a bloody lecture on it!' John paused, looking for ammunition. 'What this theatre could do with, James, is a good, thorough bloody purge of all this religious, superstitious *claptrap* everybody keeps coming out with!' He screwed up his face in disgust. 'Mascots! Magic spots!' He leaned forward and poked Fardels Bear with a makeup brush. 'Like this! Look at this! No wonder management think we're all mentally defective.' John felt he could still lay it on the line even if he did have a hangover. 'You and your sodding *Messiah*. Why can't people stand on their own two – '

'And there's no need for blasphemy,' James countered.

'Oh so you're a closet believer in the Almighty as well.' At this point even Julia put her makeup puff down and interjected 'John!'

'Just leave it, John, all right?' warned James.

'Teh! I believe! Praise the Lord and pass the biscuits!' John chanted, kicking his legs up. 'Allie-bloody-lluya! You sad sod, Mayne Young. Believes in the Almighty. Teh.'

James eyes were, for James, fairly beady and he turned them towards the door as Declan came in, dressed as Hamlet and peeling an orange.

'*Shakespeare did*,' retorted the King.

'Oh do me a favour. What, Shakespeare believed in God, now?' John was incredulous.

'There's order behind disorder in the plays.'

'Oh shut up, James. *KING LEAR?*'

'Yes, there's a divinity which shapes our ends in *Lear*.'

John kicked James's chair. 'Piss off!'

James shook his head at Declan, stood up and made a regal exit. His stage fright had vanished in a flash of genuine anger.

Padgett, who appeared to have put Declan back on his Christmas card list after last night's carousing, was confident that the Irishman would share his views on James's beliefs.

'Sad sod, he is!' John laughed. 'Reckons there's a light at the end of *Lear*. He'll be telling me about the bloody fairies next!' and with that he got up and called along the corridor: '*SEEING HE*

IS ONE!' Then he slammed the door and sat down to his makeup.

Declan was fairly subdued for a change. He had something on his mind. He looked at Padgett and looked at his orange, saying: 'He's quite right of course.'

'You *what*?'

'Nobody's ever produced Shakespeare's *King Lear* that I know of.'

'How do you mean?' said John, dropping his jaw and putting his wig on without glue.

Having seen James remedied, Julia came rushing back in to find a strange Irishman sitting back to front in her chair. She crept over to John's side, as the great man was speaking.

'Black and bleak – the "poor old bugger" treatment. Cordelia's death – the last straw. That's what most directors have done since the Paul Scofield version.'

'Yes. So?' Padgett shrugged.

'Whereas if you read Lear's death scene like a poet, which is what Shakespeare was, *that is not how it is.*'

Julia was trying to sit on John's lap.

'Get off, woman – I'm trying to wig up. I have read it, Declan. I believe I did actually peruse *King Lear* once as a child.'

'Hmmmmm.' Declan's eyes glazed over. He was deep in thought. Over the sound system came the announcement: *'Five minute call for dress rehearsal. Five minutes!*' Julia jumped up in panic, and John started doing his makeup in earnest, putting it on with a trowel.

Without looking at him, Declan tossed his orange peel at Padgett, saying: 'What do you think the sub-plot's there for?' There was no response.

'*What do you think the sub-plot of Shakespeare's play King Lear is there for?*'

Still no answer from John, who in fairness was trying to glue his wig on. Declan got up and with great violence seized Padgett by the tunic and pulled him over, tipping his chair on its back.

'Here - look out, you bloody lunatic!' John retaliated from the floor. He picked himself up and looked at the smaller man's ribs but wisely decided against it. Instead he gestured that he was trying to get made up, righted his chair, sat on it and pointed a brush at the mirror.

Declan calmly took the brush out of his hand and pulled his wig off. Julia was standing with her hands to her mouth and now looked genuinely frightened. John got up and began to struggle, which unleashed a sudden whirlwind of violence as Declan pinned him to the wall and shook him.

'You will listen to this, Padgett, if I have to nail you to a scoreboard. You annoy everybody in this theatre with your negative dogma, you know that, don't you?' Declan's extraordinary eyes blazed into John's skull. 'Why did you pick this profession if you really don't believe in anything? You're taking up a job that some real actor out there desperately wants and needs, and I object to that. I object to you freeloading in my profession. Now *listen*. *Learn*. Something about your job.'

He let John sit down.

'Just listen, darling,' Julia said gently, touching her boyfriend's hand. She could see that suddenly the gap in rank between the two male actors had yawned into a gulf and that John was about to fall down it.

'OK, OK,' Padgett sighed loudly. '*Lear*'s plot, in the middle of *Hamlet*. Let's have it.'

'Edgar finally reveals himself to his blinded father after Gloucester's torment, and Gloucester's heart, "*Twixt two extremes of passion, joy and grief, burst smilingly*." Mmmnn? Get it?' Declan's eyes were still penetrating Padgett's head. 'That's the sub-plot,' the Irishman continued, 'seeing death as a joyous release. *Now*, a lot of Shakespeare's characters manage to mumble something after they are apparently dead. Desdemona, Emilia – right? *RIGHT?'*

'Right,' said John, sounding bored to save face. Declan suddenly grabbed John's girlfriend and picked her up in his arms, Julia going quite limp with the shock.

'Now then,' Mahoney went on, his commanding voice licking the walls of the room, 'this woman appears to be dead. This woman is Cordelia and I am the King. Since the whole action of *Lear* turns on Cordelia's refusal to say "I love you" at the beginning of the play, the closure must turn on her saying it at the END. That's how poets like it. So she reveals herself to *her* father just as Edgar had done, *except that only Lear hears it!* "*This feather stirs*," he says: "*she lives! If it be so, it is a chance which does redeem all sorrows that ever I have felt*." These days, everybody supposes that the old King is rambling in his grief, here. *No.* He says, "Look on her, look, her lips; look there, look there." Because the feather is moving! Because she speaks! And *then* he dies. That's what kills him – "I love you father". *The kindness*. Sometimes death isn't a negative. Sometimes it's a victory.'

Declan gently let Julia down on her feet. 'Thank you, my little heartbreaker. Kean understood this reversal that journeymen actors like yourself, Padgett, would not have occasion to think about. Going through the looking glass.' He pointed at the mirror. 'You know what Kean wrote to his wife as an unknown, when he was starving, after he'd been turned down for every part because of his size?' He wrote: "If I should succeed now, I shall go mad." Through the looking glass.'

Seeing John put his nose to the mirror and pretend to peer in, the lights went out in Declan's eyes. Over the sound system boomed the call to arms:

'DRESS REHEARSAL. ON STAGE. ACT ONE SCENE ONE PLEASE.'

Julia was suddenly animated, fishing in her handbag for a folded piece of paper, which she held against her chest. She looked at Declan, decided, and gave it to him.

'When you have a moment. Friend of mine wrote it. It's about what you've just been saying,' she nodded. 'Read it.'

Declan stuffed the *billet doux* in his costume pocket and without comment walked out. Julia stood at the door, thinking. She was waiting for John to put his wig back on, but she was waiting for more than that.

'He's got some funny ideas, that bloke,' John mumbled. 'Missed his calling at the court of Czar Nicholas II. Professional staring done, competitive rates.'

'Hurray up, John. Last call's gone.'

'*A truant disposition, good my lord*,' John said.

'I'll go on ahead, then, shall I?'

'*A truant disposition, good my lord*.'

'John? I said I'm going.'

The door opened and Queen Gertrude peered in to chivvy them up:

'Come come come come come!' Sally chided. John turned towards them with an absent look.

'What?'

'*Now!*' yelled Sally. 'You're on! You OK Julie?' Julia nodded.

'*So have I heard, and do in part believe it,*' John frowned: '*Let us impart what we have seen tonight unto young Hamlet, for upon my life this spirit, dumb to us, will speak to him*.'

'Right, leave him, honey! He's too slow. Just leave him,' Sally called, circling her arm. John looked up again, mystified.

'What?'

'Oh bugger you then!' Julia snapped, and ran off.

'Yes, yes, yes, yes.' John was now searching in his makeup tray for something very important. He stopped, looking puzzled.

'*A truant disposition, good my lord.*'

A single bead of sweat broke out on his forehead. He looked in the mirror: his face appeared different – he couldn't figure it out. He grimaced, looking at one profile and then the other, like a man examining a strange haircut. Then he sat back in his chair.

'*'Tis strange.*'

He put his fingers up to his forehead, touched, and peered at them. Then he shook his head slightly and looked at the floor, focusing.

'*Before my God, I might not this believe without the sensible and true avouch of mine own eyes. A truant disposition, good my lord.*'

His eyes lit with fear.

'*My lord, I think I saw him yesternight.*'

He was now moving his head as though in conversation.

'*My lord, the King your father. Season your admiration for a while –* '

He broke off now, heart pounding with terror, and closed his eyes, though his lips were still moving. Then suddenly his eyes flicked wide open. He looked in the mirror and spoke quite clearly:

'Why stands thou thus amazed, Horatio?
Knowst not, as is very palpable to sense,

'Ere harbingers do swarm the black of night
To squeak and gibber like the sheeted dead
When headless Rome stood 'prised of Julius' fall,
Thy Prince the Dane hath urgent need of thee?
Why standst thou lumpish? Steel thy eclipsed soul
And go to Hamlet. Tell him what thou see'st,
Though like a soldier sent on hope forlorn
To bring ill tidings of a vanquished guard,
Hi thee, perdu, unto thy reckless lord!'

No one had ever accused Padgett of being a great actor, so it was uncanny that Horatio's lines tripped off his tongue so easily and fluently, and that they carried with them all the echoes of emotion and gesture that real words carry with real people. Then having said his lines, he got up and ran out of the dressing room.

It was rather mysterious that Padgett had suddenly mastered these lines from Horatio, because certainly none of Shakespeare's audiences had ever heard them before. It was another mystery that Padgett's dressing mirror bore within it, for the blink of an eye, the image of Edmund Kean.

Chapter Sixteen

Declan was in a London cellar tavern off Fountains Court. It was late lunchtime, and the actor was trying to wash the recent dress rehearsal out of his system using his usual method of drowning certain parts of his brain. He was expected to go back to the theatre later to help Dan Loxley sort out the problem of John Padgett's nervous smash-up.

It was a disaster for the production, a disaster for Dan Loxley's reputation and a disaster for Declan personally, for it had driven Hamlet even further away from his grasp. First Night was imminent, and amid heightened publicity the cast were about to be critically coddled.

There was also the possibility that Harvey Burns, who was going to take a bath on the production, would sue, naming Declan along with all his other British incompetents. Even leaving aside the possibility of a gigantic attack of stage fright, Declan thought, it was *not* going to be all right on the night, and he himself, normally able to defend his flank with talent and repartee, would finally be exposed 'stark bollock naked'.

Declan was beginning to feel himself under siege and overmatched. He had been up all night prior to rehearsal, drinking and arguing bitterly with one friend after another who had failed to understand his personal agony. Even his latest off-the-peg model girlfriend, sporting four finger bruises on her upper arm from a rough grab, had got a cab home.

The Irishman was alone apart from the occasional well-wisher placing drinks on his table. Two barmaids were tittering and polishing glasses. He had been reading the racing results, but he stopped and took out his wallet, pulling from it a piece of folded paper, which he opened and read.

'Look on her lips, look there, look there!
The rising and falling of her feather breath,
The rise of pity as she sucks you in,
The fall of fear to wash you back again –
It is there, the tide out of space and time,
The cast of the pearl eye, beautiful, sublime,
The rising and falling of her gentle breast –
Look there
And break your heart
And take your rest.'

The words seized his imagination like a good script. They engaged his actor's intelligence, and not just because of the scene that had just been played out in Julia's dressing room. Declan was often drunk or drugged. He often gave in to excesses and struck his enemies as a mere ego-manic lout, a hell-raiser who should have stayed in Hollywood while he had the chance, and burned himself out with his fellow dissolutes. But Declan for all his weaknesses was perfectly serious about his craft, and though he was not an academic like Loxley, he revered the theatre and had read everything he could lay his hands on about great acting.

On this piece of paper in front of him, Declan could see Cordelia's breath stirring the feather in her father's hand. King Lear was about to die on the stage, hearing her whisper her love for him at long last. It brought to a great tragedy more than solace or revenge: it brought *closure*. It expressed what Declan had been trying to drive into Padgett's skull in the dressing room: that the end of *Lear* had nothing to do with dreary pessimism or sadness as everybody supposed. It was more like a Near Death Experience, a beatific calm.

Declan had another thought about this poetic missive, too, one that was less to his liking. *Somebody had been spying on him*. Somebody had seen inside his head. And this somebody evidently had a theatre education and understood about 'pity' and 'fear' on the stage.

Like any half-decent Shakespearean actor, Mahoney had read Aristotle on dramatic tragedy. Over two thousand years ago, Aristotle had understood the actor's work. The Greek genius wrote that the whole point of theatre was to put the audience through an arts experience, one that would change and purge them. He had divided the Drama into four parts: *protasis*, the showing of the characters; *epistasis*, the working up of the plot and expectations; *catastastis*, the climax or height of the play, and *catastrophe*, or unravelling, in which everything is resolved and settled. To allow this sequence to happen, Aristotle explained, the dramatist must arouse two chief emotions in the audience: Pity, to draw them towards the hero and the action, and Fear, to repel them.

These opposite emotions built the necessary tension in the theatre to keep the audience on the edge of their seats, unable to look comfortably at the action yet unable to leave.

The tension was needed to produce the desired climax and resolution, after which members of the audience went away purged of their emotions and at peace with themselves. This ennobling experience Aristotle named *catharsis*.

Declan knew this, and so evidently did the person whose work was in his hands. It was signed 'Stencie Smith'.

***

Loxley was on the phone in the theatre's administrative office, trying to postpone a peak time chat show that he and Mahoney were supposed to grace that evening. His face was reddening because this was more of Harvey's doing and he had argued against it from the first, saying they were too near the First Night knife and would be far too tied up with rehearsals. Loxley was seething through his smile, his voice tightly controlled. This could all screw up big time.

'Yes I *know* it was arranged for us to do the *Chat to Chantry* show tonight, yes, but we're extremely busy with rehearsals.... No, I'm not saying we *cancel* it – we're very grateful for the TV exposure for the production, of course. What I'm suggesting is, we *postpone* till after First Night when we can...I'm sorry? No... Yes.... No. You couldn't do it next week?.... Oh I see. You would need both Mr Mahoney *and* myself? Well that's...Oh I see. Oh. I see. No, no. Right, we'll keep it as it is then. Right. OK. Cheers for now.'

Dan rang off and kicked the desk mouthing '*Shit!!*' He slammed out of the office and marched towards the dressing rooms, almost decking his leading actress coming the other way. She had just left Stence outside in her clapped out Mercedes.

'Where's Dec?' Loxley glowered, as though it were all Julia's fault.

'He's on his way. I wanted to ask –'

'Sally's trying to get Harvey not to cancel,' Dan said through gritted teeth.

The two of them strode towards Julia's dressing room where James and Sally were already waiting. Mrs Loxley sat with a mobile plastered to her ear and was smoothing and pleading in her finest drawl to her fat cousin. The others were at panic stations.

'Perhaps he just has a touch of the sun,' James offered, and immediately wished he hadn't.

'*Touch of the sun?*' scowled Dan. 'Touch of the fucking son of York, more like. Eh, Julia?'

Sally made a kissing noise into her mobile and switched it off.

'Now Danno,' she oiled, 'don't get upset tonight. You have that TV – '

'Sally – would you just - JULIA!' Dan bellowed.

Julia recoiled. 'I don't know.'

'*YOU DON'T KNOW – I THOUGHT YOU LIVED WITH THE BLOKE.*'

The whites of Dan's eyes were mapped with blood. He began tearing drawers off their runners and pulling open cupboards, helped by his wife, as James stood limply by.

'I do live with him,' Julia retorted.

'But you don't know anything about him – is that what you're telling me?'

'I'm not his mother. John's private. You're the one who's supposed to be *in loco parentis*.'

'I don't know him – I only employ the berserk *bastard*,' Dan spat. They all turned to see Declan make his late entrance and lean against a worktop with his arms folded.

'He's never said anything to you about this, James?' Dan needled, slamming a cupboard.

'About bringing stuff back from his holiday?'

'*Yes!*' Sally chimed in, looking pointedly at Declan.

'No,' protested James. 'He'll be all right, Dan.'

'He will be OK, honey,' Sally soothed. 'I gave him a Selzer and a double expresso.'

Julia bridled. 'He's not *drunk!*'

Sally's maternal instincts rose to fever pitch.

'We've gotta all calm down, here. Don't let's spoil the show now after all the hard w – '

'Oh he's not drunk,' Dan slammed a drawer into its socket. 'That's a relief. So long as he's only on something harmless like Crack or Mescalin, that's put my mind at rest knowing he's stone cold fucking *SOBER*.'

For the first time, Julia rounded on the director.

'*He's sick, Dan!*'

'I'm sick,' he retorted.

'He is sick,' Sally nodded, endorsing her husband.

'*Oh for God's sake!*' Julia yelled at Dan's back, as suddenly he turned round towards her with the full force of his temper, rocking his unsuspecting wife on her heels.

'*Look Julia, you ignorant sow,* all I *needed* to put the last nail in the coffin of this production was to have one of my leading actors high as a kite and out of his fucking mind *NOW – WE OPEN TOMORROW NIGHT – you got that? WE OPEN TOMORROW NIGHT* – and then to top it off what I need is for you to be standing there like the talentless tart you are, trying to tell me he's on Incapacity Benefit *with a fucking MENTAL CONDITION!'*

Throughout the storm, Declan sat on the worktop next to Fardels Bear, his blue eyes fixed on the floor, deep in thought. Dan continued raving:

'Where's that sports bag he brought back? What's this? What's in here?' He rifled through the costume cupboard.

'Shirts,' Julia answered, her face flushed with fury. 'He's not shooting dope, Dan. Christ, I live with him – I'd know if he were taking something like that. It's not John.' They all looked at Declan.

'Look,' glowered Dan, 'I don't give a shit what you piss-heads take at your own legless and topless bloody parties, but not in the theatre, and not in the middle of my fucking production. This is the theatre! This is my fucking church! Here at least I expect you to behave like a set of responsible self-catering fucking adults!'

Suddenly Julia sprang at him and screamed in his face:

'HE'S HAD A BREAKDOWN, DAN - what's the matter with you? I thought you knew all about that subject!'

'Oh my Gahd,' said Sally, turning away. Dan put his arm around his wife and looked at Julia with loathing.

'You have to have an imagination to qualify for a personality crisis,' he sneered.

'*YOU BASTARD!* You callous bastard! You and your cardboard cut-outs. *What do you think actors are, Dan?* What do you think we are? You and your precious play! All you ever see is the tops of people's heads moving about in your damn production. Well, I hope this one does something for your reputation as a director. I hope you stink from here to Stratford!'

She picked up her bag, her tears spotting the pink leather.

'Julie?' James spoke softly, trying to hold her.

'Leave her alone,' Declan said, and Julia shook herself free.

'Go to hell!' she sobbed, and hurried out.

Dan left a short pause, then added:

'Nice to see her spots have cleared up, anyway.'

'And Sal's,' echoed James.

'Oh, and yours, sweet pea.'

Dan rubbed Sally's hair. Unable to turn up the dope that might have assuaged his real fears, he sat down, visibly shaken.

'Who's understudying Padgett, Dan?' James asked.

'Sherwood. Six foot six, legs like sticks, costume, costume, costume.' He looked at his watch: 'Right.'

'How long have we got?' said Declan.

'Twenty-six hours, fifty-five minutes and about ten seconds.' Sally gave a little scream and ran out.

James's stomach dove like a plane.

'Oh God,' he moaned, 'Well, I'll be in the bar if you want me. Declan - if you need a friend. Or under it. Break a leg, dears.'

***

Outside the theatre, Stence was about to drive off from her illegal parking space when Julia came running back across the road at last with a tissue to her nose. Stence opened the passenger door and the actress jumped in and held her hands over her mouth. Then she nodded. Stence drove round the corner heading for the residential area at the back of the theatre. There she parked under a tree and turned off the ignition.

'That went well, then,' Stence said. Being just a getaway girl, she was not even wearing her wig.

Julia's nose and eyes were pink.

'That *shit.* It was unbelievable. He still thinks poor John must be stoned.' Julia blew her nose. 'The bastard just went up in there like Mount Vesuvius.'

'Directed at the whole cast?'

'No, just me.'

'Why *you?*'

'Because I live with a man who rained on his parade, I suppose.' Stence narrowed her eyes.

'Well, at least you were ready this time, Julie. Since Harvey tightened up stage door security on the press I wouldn't have got in there with *pince-nez* as Sigmund Freud.' Then she smiled. 'Was it turned on?'

'I think so.'

Julia pulled the tiny tape recorder from her handbag. 'I've been carrying it around for three days, turning the tape over and replacing the batteries like you said. I thought I might just get a lot of Shakespeare.' Stence took the little recorder, rewound for a second and pressed playback. James's voice could be clearly heard saying '*Julie.*'

They listened to the tape and agreed to meet up later to discuss their next move. Recording famous directors without prior permission might be illicit, but whether it was actually illegal in the eyes of libel lawyers remained to me seen.

***

Declan and Dan were in a limousine bound for the BBC studios in White City. They were suited and booted and had been asked to keep the tone light for the early evening family chat show slot that went out live at 7.00pm.

'You don't really think that was a dope trip, do you Dan?' Declan said, straightening his Garrick Club tie.

'Yes. No. I don't know. I don't know what to think of what's going on at the moment, Dec, to be honest. I think he's probably gone round the twist. I expect I'll see him round there myself very shortly. I don't know. What do you think? One minute John's John, and the next he's catatonic, can't hear what you're saying – like a bloody zombie.'

'Oh that's no zombie,' Declan muttered, pursing his lips.

'No?'

'It's Horatio.'

'Do what?'

'Vivien Leigh, hanging upside down in her stairwell telling visitors she's Blanche DuBois. He's retreated into the character. It's an occupational hazard.'

'You serious? *Padgett?*' spluttered Dan: 'There's something faintly sinister about that comparison somewhere.'

'*A truant disposition, good my lord,*' Declan recited.

'Don't you bloody start.' Dan looked intently at his principal. 'Dec – are you thinking what I'm thinking?'

'I doubt it.'

'Do you think this has anything to do with – you know.'

'In what way?'

'I don't know,' said Dan, searching his mental archives: 'A curse, say – like MacBomb?'

'I think he's had a breakdown,' Declan announced, shutting down the subject. Dan brightened.

'Well, I suppose I'd better text and apologise to that cow. Anything I can say to lower your spirits?'

'We'll survive.' Declan seemed abrupt, as though something had touched a nerve. Dan patted his knee as they got out of the car at the BBC.

'Break a leg. Good boy,' the director said.

Declan had privately made up his mind to go back to the Padgett dressing room in the morning. There was something he wanted to look into.

Chapter Seventeen

The black-walled BBC television studio, its floor snaking with cables, reminded Declan of a particular public school rackets court where he had once fallen asleep after a tippling actors' masterclass.

Technicians crept about like cockroaches in the anonymous dark while banks of lights blazed at the seated studio guests. It was 7.40pm London time, they were the anointed celebrities of the evening, and they were powdered, primped and paraded in front of the cameras for poor obscurities eating their dinners in their living rooms. 'Gods of the chat show sofa', Dan whispered to Declan before they were introduced.

'My final guests,' smiled permatanned show host Troy Chantry, 'are about to wow London with the most talked-about production of Shakespeare's *Hamlet* since the 1960s - and I hear those black market stalls tickets are now changing hands at 1200 quid, ladies and gentlemen, if you at home fancy a night out. So would you please welcome the play's director *Daniel Loxley* and that *fulminating* Celtic star of stage and screen, *Declan Mahoney!*'

Egged on by the waving arms of a production manager, older members of the studio audience burst into 'spontaneous' applause while ranks of young girls screamed lustingly.

'So Daniel, if I may start with you: Shakespeare – dead and rotten?'

'Not according to London's stage fans, Troy – our sponsors, Harvey Burns Incorporated, are extremely pleased with the response.'

'Well he got the plug in there right at the beginning,' Chantry exclaimed, his whitened teeth gnashed in a grin. 'But are they genuine Shakespeare fans, Daniel, or are they simply here to see that so-called *Mahoney effect* on the great Bard's efforts?' (A few sporadic screams echoed round the studio.)

'Well I'm tempted to say "Who the hell cares?"' Dan shrugged. 'After all, if we bring Shakespeare to the masses, we're carrying on the excellent work of people like Lilian Baylis at the Old Vic and Sadlers Wells years ago, aren't we? But no – this is a serious production, Declan's a serious actor and *Hamlet* is a serious play for our time, for all time. It's a psychological drama, and I think that's the appeal.'

Chantry turned to his other guest, whose eyes glittered dangerously in the lights.

'Is that right, Declan – *Hamlet*'s a head play?'

'Hamlet's a head case,' said the Irishman. 'The play, if you're interested, is about a man having a nervous breakdown.'

The phrase 'if you're interested' raised Chantry's chin bristles.

'And why would anybody want to look at *that* for 1200 quid a shot when they can go round to any London office and watch their stress levels go off the scale?' The famous pomaded hair of the show-host flopped forward with streetwise energy and wit.

'The *great Bard's efforts*, as you put it,' replied Declan, 'are about exposing human nature under the knife.'

'And is the actor then exposing *himself*?'

Chantry's gimlet insights were his trademark and now he leaned forward for camera one. The odd titter blemished the audience hush.

Declan glanced at the man in front of him, who looked as though he had been basted in gravy browning and whose £1.4 million salary could have kept a few dozen decent television actors in work. He paused for effect and smiled:

'Well he doesn't need Shakespeare for that'.

The Irishman got out of his seat and stood on the podium facing the camera with the 'on' light. Positioning himself for maximum effect, he undid his Armani jacket and proceeded to unzip his flies. Chantry leapt up laughing and grabbing the actor's arms and there was a brief scuffle.

Dan joined in, trying to separate the two men and make it look like a set piece. Some of the audience rose and pulses of outrage and titillation went round the studio in a Mexican wave. Angry exchanges broke out between a middle-aged couple and two young girls who had begun chanting '*Declan! Declan!*' and peeling off their 'Harvey Burns Inc' T-shirts. A man wearing a head mike stepped out of the shadows and signalled to the more riotous members of the audience to sit down, which they declined to do. In fact, show host Troy had some difficulty winding up the piece with aplomb and for the first time in the history of *Chat to Chantry* viewers noticed wet patches under his shirtsleeves.

Live peak time television, expected to produce the unexpected, rarely delivers genuine *frisson*. Despite the condemnation of a late night newspaper columnist and one or two programming chiefs, Declan's performance was regarded by some as having enlivened, for a few moments, the Hardly Living Room.

Certainly, Harvey Burns II lit a very fine cigar.

***

Julia had gone home to check on John, who was still staring, this time into the bathtub. Unable to get him to respond or take his prescription medication, she swore under her breath and picked up the phone, punching in Stence's number. It was the eve of the biggest stage appearance of her life, and she really needed this additional crisis. The upside was that she didn't have passive down time to get nervous.

She arranged to meet the writer for a planning supper. The venue she chose was the Gay Hussar in Soho, with its exquisite menu and cosy niches and rooms for private meetings, where they could talk quietly.

The actress was reading *The Stage* and clutching a latté when Stence rushed in, heaving a bag of papers. She was in full stress counselling regalia in case she was required to accompany Julia on official business. They knew Loxley would be on the prowl till the small hours and they had him primed for destruction. They didn't want him exploding all on his own.

'Hiya' Stence said, looking fraught.

'What's up, doc?' Julia was a gentle creature but she was also a professional, so she had refurbished herself. She was wearing full makeup and a lime green retro suit with a black clasped belt and choker embroidered with her favourite moonstones. Her blonde tresses cascaded over one shoulder and she looked a million dollars.

'You look a million dollars,' Stence commented. 'Who's coming – Colin Firth?'

'How did it go?'

'Well, it ain't good. The nationals I've talked to said yes, it's a great story and no, we won't run it without Miss Lord going on record. They're afraid of libelling the bloke, and I can understand where they're coming from but I thought they'd be willing to take a punt on a real bullying-at-work scandal like this, especially with the hype so high. They also say that our recording isn't worth much on its own because we could have doctored it. We'd have to get other members of the cast to come out against him. James?'

'James wouldn't do it,' Julia said, looking downcast at the craven state of British journalism. 'He thinks this might be his comeback role and he's desperate for the work.'

Julia was not mischievous or mercenary. But she had left her partner at home in his dressing gown staring at thin air and she firmly believed Loxley was to blame. She also believed the production should now be cancelled, Opening

Night or not, and that the director should bear full responsibility for the fiasco.

This was why she had taken a decision to invite someone else to the meeting without consulting Stencie.

'Well, we may have another string to our bow,' grinned the actress mysteriously, and called over the waiter. 'My friend would like -?'

'Oh – a pineapple juice if I may,' Stence said, now even more worried.

'I'll have another of these.' Julia pointed at her coffee glass.

'And will both ladies want a starter?' whispered the waiter.

'We won't order till we're all here.' He disappeared.

'*Not* Colin Firth,' Stence deduced. 'Oprah?'

The conversation limped along for five minutes until Julia's face lit up and she waved across the restaurant, bouncing in her seat. Stence turned round and her lungs seized.

Declan Mahoney was heading for their table. Had she known, she would have ordered a triple straight gin. Every eyeball in the restaurant had immediately swivelled, and to top it off Declan had come directly from the television studio and wasn't even late. He kissed Julia and Julia kissed him, and there were one or two luvvie exchanges that Stence didn't quite follow, and finally Declan sat down and nodded at her. This meant she was permitted to stay.

'Apparently the dailies don't want to run the story unless we get corroborative evidence,' Julia revealed. 'They're frightened of Hellboy's lawyers.'

Stence was shocked that Julia had taken the actor into her confidence. Why had she played the press card now when the reporter in question was supposed to be her therapist?

She also felt slightly betrayed. Mahoney was a very loose cannon indeed: for all Julia knew, he might decide to get matey with the director at the last minute and drop them both in the sheit. The waiter returned and almost curtseyed to the famous man in their midst. He took their orders and the meal was underway when Julia's eyes narrowed.

'Declan – why don't we just sue him for workplace stress?'

Stence had some rice on her fork that dropped down into oblivion. In her best South African accent she said:

'You'd need to involve Equity for that, and you'd have to produce the medical evidence.'

'Julia could get that from you, couldn't she?'

Declan's piercing eyes had Stence pinioned and he was watching her squirm. She stared at her plate and suddenly an image flashed into her mind of a small girl who found she could breathe again if she broke through her terror.

'Oh sod all this,' she said in her normal voice. With one hand she took off the photochromic glasses that she couldn't in any case see out of, and with the other she took a firm grip on the bobbed wig and pulled it away to reveal her own magnificent black and purple mop underneath. Then she mussed it up in its regular style: it was hers and she would do what she liked with it.

Diners on a nearby table looked carefully at their food.

'I know you disliked me on sight, Declan, but I'm not a hack. I'm a writer like I said and I've done a lot of research on your career.' She looked hard into the blue gaze. 'I believe you're a consummate actor and I think right now you have a serious director problem that will stop you doing your job. Julia's told me what happened to John. Let me do what I can. You're opening tomorrow night with an albatross round your neck. I promise you I can nail this man. Let me try.'

Declan smiled. It could well have been a smirk. Julia prodded his thigh and leaned round, wafting Estée Lauder's Youth Dew in his nostrils.

'Oh go on, Declan. *Ensemble* playing and everything.'

'I'm not an *ensemble* player.'

'Oh yes you are,' said Ms Lord, squeezing up her pretty nose.

Actually he was not, but Declan wasn't above taking advantage of the situation either. Julia was one of the most beautiful actresses of her generation and Mahoney, like a lot of male stars, had made a hobby of bedding his leading ladies.

Plus this other woman, Grub Street though she was, evidently had some insight into his work, if not the private, lonely hell that went with it.

Chapter Eighteen

The leading man and his female retinue got a cab to the Dorchester, and went up in the mirrored lift to Declan's plush suite. Stence had been on some decent interview gigs before but she had never seen anything like the four-postered, gold-brocaded and plasma-screened elegance the star had secured from Burns' beef and fag factory. No wonder he acted like a caliph when he was treated like royalty. She sat patiently at a glass table while Declan and Julia collided noisily in the dressing annex. Stence thought of Dali's painting of two lovers dining on each other's flesh with cutlery. She fixed her mind on her laptop, her dictation machine, her batteries and her tapes. Right now they were all she had.

Eventually the dishevelled thespians emerged to talk to her, which was a great sacrifice, she could tell. Of course they needed her help if she had any. They were about to go to hell in a handcart with Loxley hauling it, and what they really wanted was for her to expose him as the culprit in the press ASAFP. It might just salvage their reputations.

Stence had finally been stripped of her last dreams and fantasies and she was strong as a saint. She looked at Declan, sloshing his Irish whisky into crystal tumblers and thought: *You are a degraded little arsehead but I'll do this purely for your talent.*

'Just how bad is this production?' she asked.

'It has to get quite a lot better before it's just shit.' Declan was placing a drink before her, pretending to take it away and then setting it down again. Their eyes met and she had to smile.

'We heard about you cutting up rough with your editor.'

'I never touched him.'

Declan sat down next to the writer and said: 'You're very determined, aren't you?'

'You act. I write. That's what I do.'

'Why me?'

Stence laughed. 'Because you tread the high wire.'

'Between genius and insanity?'

'There are only two kinds of people that really interest me, Declan - geniuses and animals.'

'And I win on both counts,' Declan surmised.

Stence didn't answer. She was all done with cat and mouse repartee. Instead she took a gulp of whisky, which hardly hurt, and stared right back at him. Julia had reclined on the sofa knotting up her hair. Perhaps she was either embarrassed or jealous, but at any rate she broke in:

'Stence, can you actually *get* a newspaper to publish an exposé of Loxley? Only I thought you said they turned it down.'

'I can get it commissioned if you two go on record,' Stence replied without looking round.

'Can we do that, Declan?' Julia's voice was gentler than the others.

'Well why not. We'll give her some quotes. You can do it tonight, dear.' The actor was still looking at the writer. Her purple and black hair shot in every direction. Her dress sense, even in her counselling outfit, gave no hint of femininity, but she struck him as a woman who might be got out with the right tin opener.

'Why are you called "Stence"?'

'My name is Helen Constance Smith. When I started out in newspaper land I used that as my byline, and an old sub looked at my first effort and said, "She can't fucking write – maybe she can stencil."' Declan smiled and looked at the wristbands under her sleeve ends.

'And why did you try to kill yourself, Helen?'

Stence flinched. Julia's mouth opened as the actor grabbed the writer's left wrist and rolled back the elasticised wristband to reveal an ugly pink gash. He didn't need to see the other.

'Because years ago I looked in a big black hole,' Stence said.

'So now you're a poet.'

'I am.'

Declan's powerful voice had softened. He looked at her carefully and quoted an old ballad:

'O, my Helen
There is no tellin'
Why love I fell in:
The grave my dwellin' -
Would I were well in!'

The writer's eyes shone as she pulled her laptop in front of her.

'I know Edmund Kean said that,' she nodded. 'He said it to Victorian theatre luminary Helen Faucit when she was a little girl. He was walking with his Aunt Tidswell over the green at Richmond the summer he died, and two schoolgirls came running over to meet the sick actor in his fur coat and hat. His eyes were dark, "yet bright as lamps".'

Declan's face had opened up with joy as Stence continued:

'I was there myself the other day. I visited the great man's grave in St Mary Magdelene.'

'The black slab!' Declan exclaimed.

'Not much, for Prometheus.'

'Not much at all.'

'If you want me to write this piece by morning, you're going to have to book me a room. I live in the countryside.'

'Stay here,' said Declan.

'I can't.'

'Stay here.'

She shook her head, and rippled her fingernails on the lid of her laptop.

When they got to work, Julia and Declan took just twenty minutes to give the journalist their quotes on the tyrant Loxley, as they had been very well rehearsed. The writer immediately rang the night editor of the *Herald*, Simon Nations, who practically bit her hand off but said they would need the 1,000 words by 2am at the very latest. Stence told him this was not a problem: she lied.

She was booked into a room on the floor below. There she looked round, threw her keys on the bed, opened her laptop and staggered sideways. She never normally drank spirits and she was sick tired. Her brain was swivelling on its stanchion. An image kept flickering into her mind of the famous film star Declan Mahoney, leaning round the door of his hotel suite saying 'Goodnight Helen. *Stay.*' She had felt quite sorry for him.

Now she was forced to focus, and when she looked at her watch a wave of fear surged through her insides. It was just after midnight. She had two hours to produce a front page 1,000-word article for a national newspaper, a far more heavyweight publication than the *Sunday News* and with far more and better readers, as the *Herald* boasted several major journalists on its payroll.

Actually she had less than two hours. In that time she also had to transcribe the interviews from her dictation machine before she could begin the labour of creation. The quotes had to be slotted appropriately into the piece as she went along and she couldn't write 'blind': she had to have the actors' statements in front of her to organise her argument.

After forty minutes of scribbling she got up and rushed into the bathroom to kneel at the toilet bowl, ill with tiredness and whisky. *I can't do this* - the words of doom came up from her guts. It wasn't just the time pressure or the assignment or the fact that Loxley's lawyers might savage everything she said. What she wrote might alter the fate of the play, or the fate of the actors who trusted her. It was too much responsibility.

And underlying all these other fears, there was the fear that if she failed, Declan might think badly of her. She washed her face and sat down at the laptop, staring at the blank screen. At least her fingers worked:

'The Opening Night of *Hamlet* at the Theatre Royal, Drury Lane will be marred...'

No. Reporter rubbish. This has to be a crusading piece. She tried again:

'Dictatorship is not dead. It lives and breathes in the person of...'

No.

Stark terror is always lurking at a writer's elbow. It sits there waiting for her to screw up with a few false starts when she is under time constraints, and then it spills out from the hypothalamus and floods her brain so that she can't think, can't write, can't function. A deadline is exactly that: you write to the line or you're dead, cut off without mercy, another writer starving in a garret. The terror therefore had to be kept at bay. *Get on with it, you cow. Where's Alph when I need him? Help me. Help me*.

Then quite suddenly, at the climax of panic and adversity, Coleridge's sacred river from *Kubla Khan* began to flow, and Helen Constance Smith began to write:

THEATRE TYRANT AT WORK:

Theatre Royal actors accuse director of workplace bullying

Stencie Smith

In our democracy, forested from end to end with workplace legislation to protect employees from bullying, despots still roam the land. The majority of people who toil in their employ spend much of their time unemployed. They are consequently so grateful and desperate for work that they are willing to tolerate the most degrading treatment in order to retain their positions.

These workers are not illegal immigrant cockle pickers, enslaved girls drafted in for the sex trade, or factory surfs building computer motherboards. They are in one of the most important branches of the arts, and we rely on their talent and occasionally their genius to transport us into other worlds and engage our deepest emotions - every time we go to the theatre.

Our stage actors are in crisis. They are being exploited, they are being compromised, and above all they are being bullied. One cogent example of this new brand of workplace shogun theatre is the latest super-hyped production of *Hamlet*, which opens tonight amid enormous tumult and fanfare in London's Catherine Street, WC2 at the Theatre Royal, Drury Lane.

The play has been bankrolled by American multinational giant Harvey Burns Incorporated, a departure in the way of sponsorship for arts productions. Chief executive Harvey Burns II has gained entrée into theatreland under the banner of his meat marketing brands, but the Burns billions were made in the 1980s from the sale of tobacco products, in particular to the Third World.

Burns chose for his *Hamlet* director Daniel Makepeace Loxley, 56, the Oxford-educated theatre guru and academic whose name was made largely in New York with his award-winning productions of Shakespeare, Christopher Marlowe's *Tamburlaine* and more contemporary works like *Equus* and *Death of a Salesman*.

Among modern directors Loxley has an unrivalled knowledge of Shakespeare, but even according to his admirers his style is uncompromising. According to his detractors it is autocratic.

Last night in an exclusive interview, the two principal members of the cast of *Hamlet* revealed just how overbearing are Loxley's methods. Firebrand Irish actor Declan Mahoney, who stars as the Prince, told me: 'Daniel rules his productions with a rod of iron. Anyone who disagrees with him gets very short shrift. I've heard him ball out performers for tiny infringements and send them away in tears. It's actually counterproductive, because he is destroying the very fabric of confidence and sensitivity that enables actors to do their jobs.'

Leading lady Julia Lord, who plays Ophelia, confided that she came close to breakdown after a drubbing received at Loxley's hands during rehearsals for this play. 'I almost reached the point where I couldn't continue. My mother is gravely ill, and in one rehearsal Mr Loxley said that I should capitalise on this to improve my acting. He used the words: "Think of your fucking Mum." I cannot forgive such abuse of professional people in a theatre.'

Members of the cast allege that they are routinely spoken to like children and that they have been terrified, threatened and subjected to foulmouthed abuse. Vulnerable individuals have suffered behind the scenes from anxiety attacks and worse as a result of their inhumane treatment.

One casualty of the alleged workplace dictatorship is Julia Lord's partner, Yorkshire actor John Padgett, whose credits include *Rudy's Way* and *Make Matters Worse.* Mr Padgett, due to play Horatio in tonight's performance, is unable to attend the Opening Night at Drury Lane on medical grounds. He is recovering at home after having been found at the theatre in 'a cataleptic state' and unable to communicate.

Said Ms Lord: 'John's spirit been broken and I regard Daniel Loxley as personally responsible. He has been given far too much power over our lives.'

The British concept of a producer, or 'director' as the position has been termed in imitation of the Americans since the Second World War, is relatively new. In the nineteenth century there was no such orchestrating figure in the theatre, and actors were entirely responsible for their own performances, good or bad. They offered their services to theatre managers and received contracts according to their talents.

Consequently their insights into the characters they played were largely their own. Actors would even receive applause for their stage business and flourishes, known as 'points', which became the trademarks of their particular interpretations, and some actors commanded huge followings and managed their own theatres themselves.

With the advent of film production came the need for someone to co-ordinate the actors' performances and in England, theatre directors emerged from academe with strong theories of what theatre and acting should be.

Many were influenced by German playwright Berthold Brecht, who in his *Messingkauf Dialogues* set out his vision of modern theatre and argued that actors' powers to move an audience should be kept under very tight control.

Brecht had witnessed German dictator Adolf Hitler at first hand, and was wary of the actor's mesmeric abilities.

He thought audiences should be deterred from identifying too closely with the people on stage and used what he called 'alienation effects' such as placards and commentators to remind theatregoers that they were merely watching a play.

According to Brecht's enormously influential theory, only the action mattered. The actors did not.

Place a man, usually an academic, in charge of an entire cast on a stage, give him command of the actors' performances and ultimate control of their visions and skills, and tyranny is only a short step away.

As Declan Mahoney put it: 'Acting is an imaginative job. It is not like bricklaying. The actor uses himself, his experience, his insights, his body and his senses in order to bring the playwright's character to life. He is not helped in this tremendously difficult work by somebody bellowing at him like a serf.'

Tonight when *Hamlet* opens at the Theatre Royal, audiences will see for themselves the director's version of Shakespeare's poetic imagination.

They will see parts interpreted and characters played according to the tastes and references, not of the players themselves, but of one man: Daniel Loxley.

Whether such a man has the right to humiliate and bully professionals who have dedicated their lives to the craft of acting, and whether such theatre can be either satisfying or successful, will be judged tonight.

As Stence finished the piece she hardly had the energy to smile, but she hoped and believed it might be what they called a scoop.

She sent her 1,039 words off into cyberspace at three minutes to two and, without taking off her clothes or shoes, lay back on the bed and fell sound asleep.

***

Upstairs in the hotel, Julia fell into Declan's arms and sank down into shameless helplessness. While her lover John Padgett sat somewhere in Chiswick staring at the wall or into their bathtub, his partner was kissing Declan's shoulders. She kissed his hair, she kissed his eyes, she kissed his feet and his hands.

He carried her into the bedroom and spoke not a word as he dined on her beauty and grace, emptying himself of some of his carnal appetites as he often did prior to a major performance.

When she eventually fell asleep he got out of bed and went through her coat and handbag.

It wasn't there. And nor, although sometimes he knew she borrowed it from its hook, was the key to her dressing room.

Chapter Nineteen

A grey dawn broke on the day of *Hamlet*'s opening and spread its mists across Harvey Burns' Sussex estate. A thin rain began to speckle the lake as a heron took off from its feeding, its huge wings rhythmically flaying the air.

Over on the croquet lawn, the bust of Antoninus Pious suddenly juddered slightly, tipped and fell forward from its plinth, crashing in several pieces on the crazy paving. The noise alerted four gigantic German Shepherds who flew out over the green barking and slavering, and then stopped in their tracks, their hackles high.

Unable to understand what sort of dawn raid this was, or what sort of burglars they were dealing with, the great dogs backed away, lowering their heads and uttering small whinnying cries of fear.

In his king-sized bed Harvey Burns rolled over to speak to his wife of a pain in his shoulder, but no sound came. He died of a massive heart attack at exactly 7.00am on Friday 28th April. Just twelve hours later, his very expensive folly would open in Drury Lane without him.

When the Theatre Royal received the news it was decided almost instantaneously that the show must go on: indeed, Burns' son and heir Harvey III insisted upon it. An announcement would be made before the curtain and a floral tribute would be presented to Mrs Sally Loxley in honour of her cousin. Sally, who was born tough, would shed her tears at the appropriate time.

The final full dress rehearsal was scheduled for 9am but went ahead at 9.30am. As this production of *Hamlet* was practically uncut, it ran to almost three and a quarter hours. This meant that the early start was necessary to accommodate lunch and afternoon down-time for the players before tonight's gruelling performance.

Normally final dress rehearsal would have occupied the previous evening, but on Harvey's insistence the slot had been commandeered by live television and *Chat to Chantry*. It caused Dan Loxley a great deal of heart searching, though in fairness this was mostly of other people's hearts rather than his own.

Not a moment too soon, the cast were in full Elizabethan costume rather than the token garments they had been wearing for previous dress rehearsals. The mini-disc orchestration was filtered through the sound system, the completed sets had been sawed and hammered through the night by sweating carpenters working against the clock. The last of Loxley's chalk blocking marks had finally been replaced on the stage by items of furniture, which made a huge difference to the actors' conception of their movements and should have happened at least a week before.

The sound effects were in, the lighting plot was designed and running, the sound cues were all in place and the stage manager Duncan Frith and his assistant had largely taken over from the director, who sat in the stalls gnawing his lip, his mission supposedly accomplished.

Now more than ever, Dan regretted allowing the late lamented Harvey to bully him about the need for previews. *Of course* they had needed previews, preferably a week in the provinces, to iron out the glitches and give the actors some confidence. Burns' favoured expression 'on the hoof' might serve for beef cattle, he had told him. Dan had tried to explain to Harvey *time and again* how actors work, but the bas – the poor man wouldn't listen.

The Elizabethan costumes, painstakingly authenticated from museum exhibits and portraiture, made a huge difference to the look of the production, Dan thought. They had come in late and well over budget, with designers, embroiderers, lacemakers and craftswomen slaving over their stitching and sewing machines until well past midnight. A claw fight had practically broken out between the two wardrobe managers over Julia's £44,000 jewel-encrusted grey velvet costume for her Valentine's Day speech, and seed pearls flew like hailstones. Now, seeing their beauty in motion, the pair hugged each other in the wings.

The soft skills of the actors were very difficult to judge. They had been told not to burn themselves out prior to this evening's marathon, but Dan and Duncan were nevertheless hoping for a little more than routine avoid-the-furniture acting from the ensemble for the morning's showing.

Dan had been asked not to interfere, but his anxiety made him twist and turn in his seat. On one occasion he crossed his legs so dramatically that they brought him in physical contact with the bespectacled woman next to him, who sat with a copy of the play on her lap and occasionally looked at the director with a beady eye.

Dan did not like the psychiatric profession. He had had dealings with them in New York and had found them unnervingly expensive. Patients screamed; these guys stifled yawns and banked the cheques. His own head help honcho had sat in monastic silence while he poured out his soul, offering only conjunctive phrases like '*and how did that make you feel?*'

Now here was Julia Lord's bloody shrink, getting paid a king's ransom no doubt, and probably planning how to sue him for failing to provide a psychologically safe working environment. She had better not ask him any questions.

'Is the director's job pretty much finished now?' Dr Fay Raymond was leaning towards him and giving him the once-over with her photochromic lenses.

'That depends. I look after the actors throughout the production.'

'They need looking after?'

'Some of them do.'

'Forgive me. We haven't been introduced. I'm Dr Fay Raymond,' she said, offering her hand.

'I know who you are,' Dan nodded, keeping his hands to himself.

'You know, don't you, that Julia is extremely nervous. She has a lot to deal with right now.'

'Stage fright is normal in a theatre,' Dan shot back. 'Some actors have a bucket in the wings. The fear keys them up to deliver their performances.'

'Up to a certain level, after which it becomes incapacitating, surely.'

'You obviously don't know very much about acting. Read Stanislavski. Read Grotowski. Actors have to go into that crucible. Otherwise they are not actors: they are merely woodentops. Excuse me.' Dan got up and sat at the end of the row.

His main concern was Declan. The Irishman appeared not to have been to bed again, or not to have slept. He seemed preoccupied and was actually bloody nearly inaudible in some of his speeches. Dan realised of course that a great actor cannot give of himself except on the night in front of his audience. But something appeared to be wrong with his principal.

Had Dan overburdened him with his pages of director's notes? Had he confused him with too many directions? Had Declan's angry outburst about directors disempowering actors been a cry for help? Maybe he should have been more fatherly.

The lad might be having trouble switching from screen acting, which was small and minimal, back to stage acting which required projection and far bigger expressions. Maybe it was not too late to help him now. But Declan had *shut him out* on so many occasions.

He had refused to respect him. He had kept banging on about Edmund Kean. He had caused strife between Dan and Sally and between Dan and Harvey. Indeed, he, Loxley, had been

Declan's only real champion, if only the man could see it above his own ego.

When the rehearsal ended Dan stood up, unaccountably cheering and whistling. He called Declan over and grabbed him by the shoulders as though trying to squeeze some life into him.

'Well done, young man!'

'In what way?' Declan answered, avoiding his gaze.

'I was impressed – you've really mastered those thought units.' Declan was taking off his gloves and pulling his ruff away from his neck while Dan continued enthusing:

'Costumes look knockout. Everybody's got the blocking and I only noticed two prompts. I think with a following wind we're going to be OK after all!'

Declan's blue eyes were vacant. He seemed not just tired but completely played out. That was bad enough.

But *then* he did something that Dan found absolutely appalling.

As the director stood there talking to him, trying to boost his confidence, his leading man went over to Dr Raymond, nodded and patted her hand! *So that was it!*

Dan realised at once that the man must have been discussing *therapy*, perhaps because he was troubled about tonight. It was the ultimate rejection by an actor he had nourished and protected all along. His director could have reassured him, could have dug him out of it, if only the man had asked. And now this!

Dan was genuinely shaken. He patted Declan's back, saying:

'You heard about Harvey.' Declan nodded. 'Absolutely out of the blue,' Dan went on. 'Sally's *destroyed*. But we'll all pull together, that's the best we can do for him. Seven o'clock we let off the big fireworks. Be in makeup *at least* by 5.30, Dec – you know the routine. Any problems, I'm here – get me on my mobile. Anything you want or need. Don't wear yourself out, mate – be back here by 5.30.'

And then he watched his great white hope disappear into the wings, with a sinking sigh.

He needn't have worried. In fact Declan had no intention of leaving the theatre at all before tonight's performance.

Chapter Twenty

Julia Lord had got through final dress rehearsal without flaring up, got out of her costumes and got a cab back to Chiswick. There she unlocked the front door and called for John darling but received no answer. Dread went through her as she ran from room to room.

'*John!!*' Her voice became distorted. She threw open doors, banging them against the walls. There was no sign of Padgett, who was on very high doses of benzodiazepines and might have been expected to sleep through the day as well as the night. Evidently he had never been in their bed, which lay undisturbed.

Julia ran back out of the front door and looked wildly up and down the street, her heart thudding. With fingers trembling she rang his mobile – no answer. How could there be? Then to her horror she thought she heard a mechanical hum coming from their garage.

'*John?!?*' She sprinted round the side of the building. In her mind she could already smell the exhaust fumes.

In the garage stood Padgett's Jeep, its engine ticking over, its headlamps striped with repair tape, its owner sitting in the driving seat. John was in his dressing gown, with his hands on the steering wheel. He was alert. Julia ran over to her partner and threw her arms round him, nestling her face against his. As she covered him with tears and kisses she distinctly heard him say:

'Suspension's shot.'

They were among the finest words the actor had ever spoken.

***

Stence's midnight article had arrived at 2am on the night editor's desk but took several hours to get through the *Herald*'s vetting process. It hadn't therefore made the early editions. The piece had had to run, like all copy submitted to a national newspaper, in the usual journalistic steeplechase. It had first to clear the initial editorial hurdle, which was a question of house style and judgement on the build-up of arguments and quotes. Then it had to jump the legal fence, which in this case had meant waking the paper's most senior lawyer for consultation with his staff. Finally it had to clear subbing, captioning and illustration. So the article might have been quite worn out and completely unrecognisable by the time Stence actually saw it on the news stands.

But there it was at midday for all to read, and she was surprised at how little it had changed.

The headline now ran:

'HAMLET' DIRECTOR FACES REBELLION

The opening sentences had been revised by night editor Simon Nations to add more impact:

> Daniel Loxley, director of the much-heralded production of *Hamlet* at the Theatre Royal, Drury Lane, is tonight facing a showdown with his cast over his allegedly high-handed methods.

But apart from that, and a few minor revisions by the legal department, it was, sure enough, her article. And as the great old newspaper flapped in her hands, she grinned stupidly at a passer-by.

Having got through the challenging journalistic steeplechase, the *Herald*'s front page article found the going from the news stands to Drury Lane Theatre relatively easy. It was transported the short distance from the news vendor's outside Covent Garden tube station under the arm of an administrative assistant, who on arriving at the theatre gave it to the assistant stage manager, who gave it to stage manager Duncan Frith, who read it, swallowed, and took it to Sally Loxley's dressing room.

There he found the eminent Daniel seated at a worktop going through his good luck messages, and Sally trying on her wig and trying to compose her tribute to her cousin.

The *Herald*, face up, was placed without comment on top of the director's cards and faxes. There was a short pause, and then all hell broke out of its moorings.

Sally, her knuckles in her mouth, ran from the room in a netted wig cap. Dan let out a cry that sounded like Lower Palaeolithic man discovering fire for the very first time and, unable to get a signal on his mobile, stormed to the front office. There he snatched the phone from a young secretary's hand and smashed out his lawyer's number.

Max Vandenblum answered immediately, having already spotted the offensive item on the news stands.

Yes, he would be right on the case, but no, at first blush, he didn't think there was a libel bone to seize upon, since Dan had gone on record elsewhere boasting of his autocratic style. Yes, he would look into the actual quotes from Lord and Mahoney.

By now the secretary had stopped typing in mid-spreadsheet in case she missed anything.

'You *what*?' yelled Dan, his eyeballs on stalks. 'What do you mean *it's not actionable*? *Hallo*?..... No, I've never heard of sodding Stencie Smith! What am I paying your legal eagles for if they can't buffer me on a libel?......Do what? Now you listen to *me!*....*You what*?....I *know* I said 'Bring me another box of actors!' at the press conference.... That doesn't make me a damn *TYRANT* does it?....No I do not bloody-well *BULLY* people!...I'm known for *what*?.... I'm a *what*?.... You *WHAT*?'

And he rang off, letting out a heart-rending scream.

Dan ran down to the dressing rooms, his face blotched with red corpuscles. He tried the door to the Number One, found it locked. He thumped and banged but without response. He went to the door of Julia Lord's dressing room and bellowed

'*Julia!*' No answer. She said she was going back to Chiswick to see Padgett, that's right.

So now he leaned with his back against the wall, his chest heaving. He would have to try to compose himself.

He had to bring the production back under his command before 7pm and straighten this out with the girl and Mahoney - no, proclaim the *injustice* in front of the entire cast, call a meeting - no, get his SM to call a meeting, and get Declan and Julia to apologise, or no, get them to *sign a statement*. Yes, get them to sign an *official statement* denouncing the article. Or call a meeting and get them to *admit* they'd libelled him, and make sure the Drury Lane manager was there to witness. Or call a press conference before the performance. Or *after* the performance.

Had Dan been slightly less panic-stricken or slightly more observant, he might have noticed two interruptions in the thin band of daylight that glimmered under Julia's door, and he might have noticed the edge of the masking tape that had been used to hold the lock in neutral after it had been opened with a credit card. Indeed, had Dan simply pushed the door, he might have felt the bodyweight of somebody holding it shut on the other side.

The burglar had been constrained by circumstances: he had been unable to procure the key by indirect means, yet he wanted to avoid alerting theatre management by asking for it in person.

His person would definitely have been recognised.

Chapter Twenty-One

Outside, the humid spring weather stifled London and thunder clouds gathered over Drury Lane. It was 3.40pm yet it was almost dark. Inside the dressing room belonging to Julia and Padgett, Declan Mahoney was on a desperate quest. He was willing to clutch at any straw, at any handhold however narrow or painful, that might save him from slipping down into the abyss of failure on the stage at 7 o'clock this evening.

The sound of Loxley's footsteps having long since faded, Declan stood away from the door and looked at his watch.

All hopes of conquering Hamlet by study or talent had at last deserted him. He knew, though he had admitted it to nobody, the part had failed to jell in his mind. Hamlet was unlike Shakespeare's other heroes in that he was neurotic. He was a man of words, many of them fearful, whereas Declan was an animal actor, pouncing and shifting, channelling his passion and intelligence. Hamlet lacked the predatory menace that was Declan's speciality. In this actor's terms, the character was insufficiently dark: a talker, a wimp.

It was easy to blame Loxley and his academic nitpicking and bullying: too easy. Quite apart from Loxley's interference, something was missing. Hamlet had simply failed to inhabit his frame. The spirit had not materialised. And there was a more disturbing thought. Perhaps he, the dauntless Mahoney, had been so deeply unnerved by what happened with Richard III that he had closed that particular valve of consciousness, that magic portal between the part and the man.

Perhaps after all, he himself was really the thing he most despised - a craven mummer, a luvvie, a line-learner.

Yet like all great actors, Declan retained a sixth sense, a vivid imagination and an open mind. Dark forces were always at work in the unlit corners of a theatre. Away from the glare of the lights, weird superstitions and paranormal events broke out and scuttled across the boards. Why, this very Theatre Royal, Drury Lane was steeped in sinister phenomena.

The oldest theatre in the world still in use, it boasted at least one ghost that was seen on a fairly regular basis, and there had been two assassination attempts in this building.

Closer at hand, something had happened to John Padgett. Declan couldn't accept the trite explanation that John had simply had a breakdown. No: some catalyst had opened that airlock between the host and the character.

Something here!

Declan's first idea had been to examine Julia's antique mascot, Fardels Bear, which was as usual sitting on her worktop. This was why he had gone down her handbag while she was asleep. He had handled Fardels before: indeed he had casually used it to clean the screen of his DVD player and thrown it at the actress in his dressing room.

He picked it up now, turned it upside down and shook it, but nothing struck him as abnormal or strange. It was just a piece of detritus from the past, an amateur's clumsy and artless rendition of a bear, no doubt made for a child. He looked at it closely to see if there were any broken seams – no. He felt it for telltale lumps that might indicate something hidden inside - nothing.

So now he turned his attention to the mirror above John's dressing table. He tapped it, looked either side of it, held a script in front of it. Reflection normal, everything normal.

He sat down in John's chair and went through his makeup tray. Nothing there either, apart from the usual powders, pastes and coloured sticks. He sat back, and his eyes wheeled round the room. The rain had begun to hammer at the window and distant thunder grumbled above the London traffic.

This had all been a ludicrous folly. He must be mad, breaking into somebody else's dressing room to examine mascots. 'Good luck', 'bad luck'! You make your own damn luck. He would go back and face the music. He would walk through his part, say the lines, stick in some voice modulations, make a few facial expressions, a few gestures. It might not be great acting but hell - they couldn't hang him for it.

He could re-lock this dressing room door as he left by pulling off the masking tape and using his thumb to slot the bolt in place, no problem. He glanced over at it now.

And as he did so, in the periphery of his vision he thought he saw a tiny movement, like an insect flickering in front of a lamp. He turned his head quickly but it was gone. Perhaps it had been a flash of lightning but he thought it had come from the direction of Julia's mascot.

He got up, crept across the room and bent down in front of it. Its tiny eyes were not the regular buttons or beads. They appeared to be made of coal, or some other dark mineral that gave off a faint but definite glimmer.

The actor was curious now. He went over to the light switch and flicked it off. It was then, as he turned towards the worktop, that he knew for certain he had not been mistaken. Because there it was again - the mascot's eyes were actually *glowing*. In fact they were blood red. The little specks appeared to be fulminating, smouldering with a fire from some unknown dimension. And as Declan stood watching like a man wrenched out of one reality and into another, the mascot gave a jolt, seeming suddenly to have been hit by an electric current.

The actor leapt across the room, turned on the light switch and seized hold of the talisman, feeling the current trace through his body. He let go and looked in the mirror, expecting to see his hair standing on end. It was not.

He picked up the Bear again, experimented, examined his face in the mirror. Then he closed his eyes, and his lips moved. He looked in the mirror, holding Fardels tightly, thinking, apparently wrestling with some mighty inner conflict.

Finally, taking the talisman and releasing the door lock, he headed for his own dressing room. He was out of earshot when the dark forces of the theatre gave a much more dramatic show of their strength.

As a thunderclap shook Drury Lane, John Padgett's mirror exploded in a shower of shards.

***

Julia got out of her cab in the teeming rain and rushed into the theatre with a newspaper over her head. It was the midday *Herald* and she had read it. She knew therefore that it would not be long before she was confronted by her director, maddened like a bull.

She picked up her key from the office and managed to make her way unchallenged to the dressing rooms, bidding good luck and 'break a leg' to other members of the cast as she checked her mobile: several messages she had deliberately ignored, including two from Loxley. She just wanted to get ready for tonight's performance without having another maiming row, and the dresser was coming in to help her in half an hour.

She put her key in the lock, swung open the door and dropped her handbag. A carpet of fragments glittered from the floor and from John's worktop. The mirror, black and empty, had gone out like a light.

Julia stood stunned for a moment before saying '*Shit!*' Then she ran back to the office to get them to clear up the mess. No, nobody *else*'s dressing room had been damaged by the thunderclap, although a couple of roof tiles slid off in the road.

It was *so* the last straw, and not the sort of luck she expected of little Fardels Bear at all. Time to bin the bugger.

Where was he, by the way?

Chapter Twenty-Two

The Theatre Royal, its entire facade lit up in the rain by red and blue lasers, was heaving. Its 2,200 seats having sold out weeks beforehand, an air of expectant rapture filled the historic building. Its auditorium was a fidgeting blaze of colour; its boxes were brimming with showbiz dignitaries.

The crowds outside in Drury Lane had stopped the London traffic for several miles around and police were struggling to move fans and *paparazzi* away from the front entrance. The red carpets were trampled and scuffed as genuine ticket holders argued with front-of-house staff while there were a good many touted or counterfeit bums on seats inside.

It was 6.50pm, T-minus ten minutes. Sally Loxley stood in the wings, having swallowed two tranquillisers and a brandy. Her magnificent burgundy Gertrude costume was embroidered with faceted beads, its starched voile collar standing high behind her beaded hair. She smiled and nodded at the ASM, but her face was white with Elizabethan chalk makeup and stark fear.

She clutched the tribute to her cousin Harvey, which she would endeavour to hide behind her back while she delivered from memory. But things had not been easy, with poor Danno in such a pitiful state.

He had been betrayed by backstabbers who owed him so much, and his temper tirades had taken their toll on the man's vitality. He was presently sitting in the wings on a plastic folding chair, his face wrought with sorrow.

He had told his wife there was little hope for this Opening Night. Declan hadn't even had the decency to emerge from his dressing room to speak to him and had admitted only his dresser, a pretty Galway Bay girl by the name of Sinead O'Casey who was suspected of satisfying his every need prior to a performance. Whatever he was doing to Sinead, Dan knew for sure that the Irishman hadn't bloodywell conquered Hamlet.

They were all about to be exposed in front of the critics who were already hostile about the lack of previews, and in front of an audience that had been hyped up by the Burns PR machinery to virtual fever pitch.

Backstage, Bernardo and Francisco, soldiers at their posts on Elsinore's Castle battlements, waited for curtain raise, Bernardo having finally sorted out the problem with his costume's crotch. His hair had relaxed; the rest of him stood to attention.

In dressing rooms and corridors awaiting their later Scene Two cues were the actors playing Polonius, Laertes, Voltimand, Cornelius, lords and attendants, and James Mayne Young in his purple kingly robes, overdosing on his nicotine inhaler, the patches having failed him. In fact only James's iPod *Messiah* feeding softly through his earphones stood between him and a fainting fit. Padgett's understudy, on the other hand, had been kitted out in extra long tights and was keen to strut his stuff.

Also required for Scene Two would be Declan Mahoney. Apart from the said dresser, nobody had seen the Irishman since four o'clock. His Number One door was locked, and although sounds were heard from inside, he refused to communicate with management staff or the SM who had several times gone down to try to talk to him.

Dan had tried whispering through the keyhole but to no avail. He understood how very nervous an actor may be prior to Opening Night. Over the years he had seen a number of famous performers, eviscerated with terror, giving up their guts in the dressing rooms or in the wings.

He knew that Declan, being a particularly courageous and daring actor, would be suffering more than most. He would pay a very high price for tonight's performance, one that would drain him mentally and physically. He was likely to be sitting in his dressing room right now in a state of semi-insanity, awaiting the moment when he faced the audience as Hamlet for the first time.

Dan knew that his leading man hadn't been able to don his character, and that he had never conspicuously failed before.

The only reasonably cheerful soul in the whole production at this point was Julia Lord. In spite of the recent thunderclap, she seemed more robust than usual and 'stress management' had very little to do with it.

In her dressing room the actress was putting the finishing touches to her makeup in her own mirror, the other having been put out like one of Gloucester's eyes. Her dresser, a middle-aged woman who rejoiced in the name of 'Dandy' Miles, was an old-fashioned cockney whose no-

nonsense humour made the actress giggle at serious times.

'Look at this luvvie's little tiny shelf!' Dandy was holding forth: 'No wonder Ophelia couldn't bleeding swim. Stuff these raw chicken breasts down your front – now don't play me up: do it for 'Amlet. You know the poor sod's radio rental over yer.'

With her Padgett on the mend, Julia's spirits had risen, and she had resisted the common temptation to have one last look at the script, as so many actors do. It would only have made her confused and nervous. She knew Ophelia. She felt she had weathered the storm, so to speak, and mastered her own modest take on the lovelorn girl she was playing.

She had just rung her mother in hospital to tell her that she had gone fifteen rounds with Dan Loxley and won on a technical knockout. Coral laughed. She always knew her daughter would make it. Julia didn't regret the loss of her lucky mascot either, and didn't particularly care who had taken him. *Love was better than luck*, she thought. Her blonde tresses were braided with pearls: Dandy said she looked a scorcher. She was to go out there and *burn 'Amlet down.*

The expectant stir out front was louder than the music. In the most expensive rows of the stalls among the actors' friends and family members sat Julia's 'stress counsellor', her journalistic mission accomplished: in fact she had received a call from the *Herald*'s features editor congratulating her on the piece and suggesting lunch. But Stence wasn't working tonight.

She had come to support her actor friends and thought they might still triumph if they went for broke. John Padgett had hoped to accompany her and even put on a suit, but at the last minute sensibly decided against it: hearing Horatio's lines might have damaged his recovery.

At two minutes to the hour the loud audience hubbub suddenly died down as Sally Loxley stepped before the curtain. She stood in solemn silence for a few moments, mercifully unaware of the presence of Ms S. Smith, hack and assassin, in the fourth row.

> *'Good evening ladies and gentlemen. We are here tonight in this historic Theatre Royal to honour the world's greatest playwright. We are also here to pay tribute to a man whose astounding generosity and deep love of Shakespeare's work has made this event possible: my cousin Harvey Burns II who –'*

At this point several theatre pundits in the front stalls squirmed and cleared their throats:

> *'- who passed away this morning, tragically robbed of his moment of glory by just twelve hours! Yet I know that Harvey would have wanted tonight's production to go ahead. It had been his ambition and his dream! The cast and those who have laboured behind the scenes, like my husband Daniel Loxley who directed and masterminded tonight's performance, share*

one hope: that we may do credit to Harvey's memory, to our sponsors, to our audience, to the critics, the media and of course the stars gathered here with us tonight –'

whereupon Queen Gertrude broke with royal protocol by mugging for celebrities and Harvey Burns III's VIP guests in the boxes:

'- and above all, ladies and gentlemen, to William Shakespeare himself. Thank you all so much!'

There was a round of applause, the digitised orchestra struck up and the curtains wound back to reveal Denmark, recreated with no expense spared, and a guard platform in front of Elsinore Castle with its flagpole and rope dangling from the gridiron. Bernardo's mouth opened successfully and the words 'Who's there?' came out. The show was underway.

The whole of the first scene went without a prompt and Tim Godsthorpe's Ghost, in soundless footwear, twice came and went according to plan.

The Scene Two actors stood silent in the wings, James having composed himself as King Claudius, Sally's Queen Gertrude pulling nervously at her bodice. Then Duncan the stage manager did a head check of the retinue and mouthed: '*Where's Hamlet?*'

In the restricted space between Drury Lane's main dressing rooms and its cavernous dark-walled stage, a figure in black velvet doublet and hose had finally emerged from the door of Number One and stood waiting for its cue. It then moved soundlessly towards the wings in its pointed black suede slippers, its shadow moving along the wall like a separate sinister creature, its long narrow sleeve flares almost brushing the ground and its black calfskin gloves clutching a silver hip flask.

The face was white, the eyes hollow and hidden, the lips gripped in a narrow smile. Reaching his spot in the wings, the man they called the Actor with the Bottle took several swigs.

He was ready.

Scene Two was set in a state room of the castle. The characters were assembled round an enormous oak banqueting table that had replaced Loxley's chalk marks, covered with flagons and goblets. Hamlet's uncle, King Claudius, fresh from the foul murder of Hamlet's father and obscenely wedded overnight to his mother Queen Gertrude, was bidding farewell to messengers.

The black velvet figure stood upstage, looking towards the wings. As the King approached him he shuddered away. Claudius was saying, 'But now, my cousin Hamlet, *and my son* –' and the audience heard Hamlet's pre-recorded 'aside' whispered over the sound system, '*A little more than kin, and less than kind*'.

Gertrude protested at Hamlet's continued mourning for his father and constant searching for him 'in the dust', and she lifted his gloved hand to her lips and urged him to accept death as they must all die. '*Why seems it so peculiar with thee?*' she asked him.

'Seems, madam! Nay, it is; I know not "seems"'.

And for the first time, the face of the black costumed figure turned towards the audience. To the front rows its eyes looked peculiar. This was because the actor was wearing white contact lenses with black centres. His speech transfixed the crowds. They had never heard a voice quite like this before. When the rest of the characters left the stage and Hamlet began his soliloquy:

> *'O! that this too too solid flesh would melt,*
> *Thaw and resolve into a dew;'*

- a woman at the end of Stence's row in the stalls passed out, and two St John's Ambulancemen quietly lifted her out of her seat and carried her towards the exit in a well-rehearsed routine.

On stage the black figure tore off the glove that Gertrude had kissed, and rubbed its hands together as though trying to remove some deadly organisms that the Queen may have transmitted to its skin. Hamlet knelt on the stage and continued:

> '*Or that the Everlasting had not fix'd*
> *His canon 'gainst self-slaughter! O God! O God!*
> *How weary, stale, flat and unprofitable*
> *Seem to me all the uses of this world...'*

The figure in black distorted his face as though fighting for control. His father had been dead 'not two months'. His mother had remarried 'before the shoes were old' in which she had followed his poor father's coffin. At *'Frailty, thy name is woman!'* the character seemed almost to retch the words on the stage.

No audience had ever seen an actor engage with Hamlet's state of mind in quite this way. They had seen technical skill, passion, even genius, but this seemed to go beyond performance or acting. It was as though Hamlet the Dane himself were writhing in fresh pain in front of them.

They were yet more surprised when in Scene IV the black clad figure, summoned by his soldier friends at night to witness what they had seen on the guard platform, encountered the dread spectre of his father.

John Padgett's understudy as Horatio, warned: *'Look, my lord, it comes.'* Tim Godsthorpe's Ghost, whom the audience had met already, began to walk the battlements. The special effects that had been conjured by Harvey's millions made the Ghost appear transparent, yet the audience knew they were watching stage trickery, smoke and mirrors.

The character of Hamlet, however, certainly did not. The black clad figure clearly believed this to be a real ghost, and its voice was suffused with alarm and emotion:

> *'Angels and ministers of grace defend us!*
> *Be thou a spirit of health or goblin damn'd,*
> *Bring with thee airs from heav'n or blasts from hell,*
> *Be thy intents wicked or charitable,*
> *Thou com'st in such a questionable shape*
> *That I will speak to thee...'*

Something was happening to the wraith itself. Although the audience knew that it must be an actor transformed by special effects, they were now less sure of their senses. To Hamlet's perception, certainly, it had morphed into something else.

The spirit of Regency tragedian Edmund Kean rose up out of the spectral form like a ghoul and placed itself in front of his whitened eyes.

Edmund Kean! But *was* this Kean? The shape seemed to be alternating uncertainly between the image of the tragedian and an absolute gargoyle. Indeed, the spectacle was so terrible that it was almost beyond the modern actor's power to remain in its presence. He wanted to flee, yet his sorrow and care for what might be Kean's ghost absolutely forbade it.

Held in suspense between pity and fear, the black clad Prince was being eviscerated on the stage. But then, as the tension became unbearable, came the tipping point: the Ghost beckoned the actor.

As the soldiers sought to deter him, Hamlet drew his sword. Purged of his conflicting emotions, the character appeared suddenly ennobled, and stood in a state of grace. Without a quaver his voice announced:

> '*Why, what should be the fear?*
> *I do not set my life at a pin's fee;*
> *And for my soul, what can it do to that,*
> *Being a thing immortal as itself?*
> *It waves me forth again; I'll follow it.*'

The soldiers again tried to lay hold of their friend, but he turned the point of his sword towards them, showing that he would protect the Ghost at all costs and follow wherever it led. And with that, both the Spectre and the Prince left the stage.

The rest of the cast, like the audience, were dumbfounded, and their jaws did not close throughout the rest of the play. Only one person in the stalls thought she understood what they were witnessing.

Although she herself could not see any metamorphosis in the Ghost, it was evident to her that Shakespeare's words had had a different meaning for the actor playing Hamlet, and that he had just played out, in front of her, an encounter with his life's great guide.

For this member of the audience, the whole scene resonated differently. This performer's Hamlet had been styled on Kean rather than Kemble: it was virulent and severe. The stage business with the sword was something the actor had borrowed from his readings of Kean's performances.

The critics would no doubt write that it was a *tour de force*, but they had written that of other actors in the part who were simply clever or gifted.

Whereas it seemed to Stencie Smith, a writer and poet admittedly obscure, that a doorway had somehow opened between the character Hamlet and the actor Declan Mahoney.

It seemed to her that Declan had been possessed.

Chapter Twenty-Three

Sinead O'Casey was an extremely pretty redhead who had visions of becoming an actress herself one day. This job was only a stepping stone. She stood with a towel over her arm in the Number One dressing room, waiting to dance attendance on the Star. He was attractive, of course, but he was unpredictable. He might come in after a rubbish evening and carry her in triumph round the room. You just never knew.

She looked up: sounds of thunderous shouts, whistles and applause echoed from the auditorium after Declan Mahoney's definitive Hamlet. Drury Lane had been rocked by a performance so mesmerising, so authentic and original that critics piqued by the lack of preview performances who had ready-penned hostile copy were obliged to bin what they had written and start again with banner headlines.

Unnoticed on the wall behind Sinead's head, the portrait of Kean flickered, vanished and reappeared as though it were being tested by some parallel universe.

The door flung open and Declan entered in costume, his pin eyes focused on the floor. Sinead followed him with the towel and a boxer-style dressing gown, trying to do her job. Declan paced round the room. Every time the dresser tried to pull at his costume, Declan turned away, glowering in concentration. Sinead pulled and pestered.

Finally Declan exploded, smacking her in the face, opening the door and bundling her out. Hearing the girl's footsteps scurrying away he closed the door again and locked it.

He then sat down at his dressing mirror and set about removing his makeup. He managed to take out the white contacts, but the rest would not come off. He rubbed and he cleansed, but without effect. The Hamlet face, which was an expression rather than the result of paint or prosthesis, belonged to Declan now. He continued his efforts, in the end making a surrealistic gesture holding the side of his face with both hands and attempting to tear it off his head. Addressing himself in the mirror he spoke:

'"Dispatch."
Canst thou not name the word? E'en so
Dost thy unsaying prove thine enmity
Unto the hottest of thy father's hopes.
Go to! Tear at this visage. Thou wast wont
Ever to flee the face of that command.
Fly, Hamlet, fly! Seek out some sharper way
To hell, which gapes to gorge itself on thee.
Forget thy loving father's sleepless sprite,
Forget thy woes, forget thy blood's revenge.
Wouldst make a period to thy mind's disease?
Dispatch the Prince. If not, dispatch the King!'

Somebody was tapping outside. It was Julia, wanting to be the first to congratulate Declan on his triumph. Finding the door locked, she whispered through the keyhole '*Let me in!*' Declan got up and unlocked the door.

Seeing Ophelia standing in the frame, his mouth fell open but he admitted her. Julia came in and stood with her hands behind her back, still touching the door handle, silent, excited, her face suffused with admiration for this man's genius. Once she began, she could not shut up.

'I have to tell you that my first reaction, my *very* first, was to hide. I was so spellbound. And I'm about to stand here now and reduce it to a rubble of words, which I shouldn't, but here I go because I've just *got* to tell you. You made my nose bleed out there – what can I – with shock and amazement at you – study and admiration of you – and despair as well, at such untouchable, unstoppable talent. Declan – you were – you were *BEAUTIFUL*. I saw it go – it travelled across the stalls and up their legs, and into their eyes, and up to their brains, delivering a fatal effect like a basilisk! Oh, everything they say about great acting is true – everything! Even about it being sexy – like a rage of sexual, predatory beauty! I shall *never* forget – *any of it!* Your eyes tonight, they were wonderful and weird – like Kean's eyes, boiling into the back row! You did it, man. You were – you were the best there is, Declan! The very best – better even than Kean, than anybody. Thank you for being born. I'm silly and stupid, I'm embarrassing, but – I just had to tell you. Thank you, Declan.'

The actor's bloodshot eyes were fixed on her. He shook his head.

'I can't get out', he said softly.

'Of course you can't – they're going to mob you out there – Dan – who's OK by the way and a bit *tearful* actually – told them all to let him come in on his own, because it's his way and he wants to have a little word with you, you know, I think to patch things up?' she was smirking, 'and after that it's Nelly bar the door – all hell's going to break loose! Simon and Bernard are down from Stratford and they've brought an –'

Declan took her by the shoulders and looked in her face:

'I can't get out.'

'Oh you can't get out! Oh I *see*. How many fingers am I holding up? You are bad, Declan – that is *so* not funny. You are an absolute worm!'

'No,' he said, shaking his head.

'What, you mean you – no?' She looked at him carefully. 'I don't understand, Declan – are you saying you normally – what are you saying? You mean you think you've got – not like John. You don't mean like John, do you?'

'*I can't get out*.'

Julia examined this face, with its front teeth clenched in a strange desperate grimace. It was not familiar.

'Of course you can't, Declan. Well, something incredible like this is bound to stay with you for a bit – like a hangover almost – I mean, it's the most amazing – of course you're in shock – a bit shocked! Like shellshock.'

She put her arm round him. 'You're all right. Talk to me! You're all right, Declan. What is it? What's the matter? Say something, come on.'

Exerting tremendous control, Declan answered:

'Verse.'

'Oh verse, yes – OK right. Yes, tell me – anything.' Declan began to recite:

'Whose shade is that? Why, it is his. It's his.
It crept up to my feet the other day,
A disembodied voice, a disembowelled past,
The calling card of someone fairly vast
(Though we were introduced in sleep
Like lovers hearing one another snore)
And suddenly a full-blown shadow broke
Across my bow, and he has caught me now,
And will not let me ACT him any more.....'

There was loud thumping. Dan Loxley stood outside with a bottle of champagne in his fist and brotherhood in his heart. Julia went over and unlocked the door, holding it ajar and whispering, '*Five minutes, OK?*'

Then she returned to the actor, who was now sitting down, as though defeated at last by a great weight on his shoulders. Julia bowed next to him:

'Declan, Declan, Declan. Come on. You're the one who's got all the angles on studying for a character and working the character up inside you, and the sweat and agony you have to go through even to get the images to stick, the ideas and clues you pick up from the writer, to make it real. It's an effort, you told me – you're making yourself available to this identity you yourself have created.

It's not a person, is it? I mean, that would be – well – it would be ridiculous, wouldn't it?'

She looked over at Esmeralda on the worktop. 'It comes from inside you – you said that, or Gielgud – that it's like a spider pulling it all out of himself like silk. It's all you, Declan. That's your job. Finding it inside yourself, some part of you that you can use.'

Declan was becoming more anguished, shaking his head.

'Him!'

'The character.'

'HIM!'

'Who? Kean? Hamlet? Who? Who's *him*?' Declan was suddenly transformed:

> '*Speak the speech, I pray you, as I pronounced it to you, trippingly on the tongue. But if you mouth it, as many of our players do, I had as lief* –'

'Declan, you're quoting *Hamlet*. Don't quote *Hamlet* at me – come on. You don't have to speak in Hamlet quotes. Talk to me! Come on – look, Dan's outside – they're all waiting – Declan! Listen, I know. *Other* than *Hamlet*, what's your biggest play – *Tamburlaine*, right? Right – Christ – I don't know a word of Marlowe, please God help me – er – "*Now, Faustus, must thou needst be damned* –" No, no, no, er –'

'*And canst thou not be saved? What boots it then to think on God or heaven?*'

'No, no, no, not that – *er* – just a second –'

'Away with such vain fancies and despair – despair in God and trust in – '

'Declan! Declan stop it, stop it!'

She was crying now, and Declan opened his eyes wide and began to recite again:

'Oh thou art fairer than the evening's air,
Clad in the beauty of a thousand stars,
Brighter art thou than flaming Jupiter
When he appeared to hapless Semele:
More lovely than the monarch of the sky
In wanton Arathusa's azure arms,
And none but thou shall be my paramour.'

Julia brightened.

'That's better! Now do Richard. Come on – *"Death, desolation, ruin and decay..."*'

'It cannot be avoided but by this;
It will not be avoided but by this.
Therefore dear mother –I must call you so–'

But the reference to 'mother' sprung a hair trigger in his brain and he returned to *Hamlet*:

'But by this hand is my confounded soul
Come forth to shake the superflux with me
And make me mad indeed!'

Julia seized him in her arms. 'You're not mad, Declan! You're not mad. You're not going to be mad. You're going to be fine, just fine – now look at me.' Declan nodded and returned to Richard's speech:

'*It cannot be avoided but by this –*' He was struggling:

'*Whether 'tis nobler in the mind –*'

Julia shouted:

'*NO!* You're quoting *Hamlet* again Declan, now stop it!' She slapped him. *'STOP IT!'*

'Julia. Julia, it's Julia.'

'Yes that's right, it's me, Julia. I'm here, Declan. I'm here and I'm going to stay here with you, and I'm not going to leave you for a second, and I'll eat with you, and sleep with you and I'll even go to the toilet with you because I love you and you're going to be all right. That's it.' She began to rock him in her arms. 'That's it.' She was humming. 'That's it.'

'It wasn't me,' Declan said. 'I don't remember any of it.'

'Poor Declan. Poor, poor Declan. What am I going to do to put you back together again, eh? Humpty Dumpty sat on the wall...'

'Humpty Dumpty had a great fall!'

'That's it. You OK? You know *why*, Dec? Because of all this Irish Catholic *stuff* – all that guilt your race has been carrying around with itself for centuries about original sin, and hellfire and damnation. You gave a tremendous performance and you think you've been too proud and you've got to be punished for it. You think you've got to pay for it.' She sat on his knee.

'That's it, is it? Guilty conscience.' He laughed.

'That's right. I see it was you who stole my Fardels Bear, as well – a hanging offence. I thought he'd grown legs and walked away. Declan – you're a great actor. You're great, and brave, and I love you.'

'That's very good.'

'You all right, now? Sure? Can Dan come in – God knows what he thinks is going on in here. If you're decent, Mr Mahoney. I'll let them in now, shall I, good my lord?' Declan nodded.

'Guilty conscience.'

Julia turned away and opened the door. As she did so, Declan's expression changed.

'*Nymph, in thy orisons be all my sins remembered.*'

Dan Loxley strode into the room looking slightly put out, but buoyant nonetheless.

'What was all that about?' he laughed.

Julia was looking at the actor, who had stood up.

'Declan?'

'*Get thee to a nunnery. Why wouldst thou be a breeder of sinners? I am myself indifferent honest, but yet I could accuse me of such things that it were better my mother had not bourn me: I am very proud, revengeful, ambitious, with more offences at my beck than I have thoughts to put them in, imagination to give them shape, or time to act them in. What should such fellows as I do crawling between earth and heaven? We are arrant knaves all; believe none of us. Go thy way to a nunnery!*'

Three or four members of the company had joined the director. Sally Loxley and Tim Godsthorpe stepped inside the doorway along with Padgett's understudy and one or two Extras and well-wishers. Declan, seeing the assembly, broke off and pushed his way violently through the throng, making his way through the theatre's innards.

They all stood in amazement. Julia understood exactly what had happened and Dan quickly cottoned on. He banged down the champagne next to Fardels Bear and grabbed his mobile.

'It's got him - shit. I knew it,' he said quietly.

'*It's got him?*' Sally looked bemused. 'We got a glitch here, honey? What the hell is going on? Danno. Danno?'

'I knew it. I knew it,' Dan was saying, punching the buttons and unable to get a signal.

'Daniel – it's not your fault,' Sally intervened. 'The guy's whacko. He's got you spooked! He's a soak – we all knew that. Harvey said the guy would freak –'

Dan had grabbed her shoulder, realising what Declan's next move might be.

'Sshhh! Shut up, shut up. If he thinks he's – where's James?'

'Where's *James*?' Sally wondered. 'What the hell has James got to do with it?'

'*Claudius*!' Dan said through gritted teeth.

'Holy Joe's pyjamas!'

They all rushed out of the room. And nobody noticed, there in the champagne bottle, two small, red reflected lights from another world.

Chapter Twenty-Four

James no longer drank. Post-match celebrations held no charm for him these days. He had already changed into his day clothes, thrilled that he had been part of such an overwhelming piece of theatre but discombobulated by the adrenaline rush and worried about tomorrow's equally gruelling performance.

It was past 11.30pm and he was making his way to his Volvo in a side turning when he caught sight of somebody running, apparently in his direction. As the figure drew nearer he could make out who it was. Declan – and still in costume in civvy street! He must be bladdered already. James saw something shiny in the actor's right hand and thought he was carrying a bottle. In fact it was a stage property – a vial that had been used in the scene depicting Hamlet's father being poisoned.

'Why, it's the star himself! Congrat – '

Mahoney leapt towards him with maniacal force and seized him by the collar, wrenching on his neck and tipping liquid in his ear. James was bigger than the Irishman and stood up, breaking his grip.

'What the hell –'

Declan looked at him in anticipation, then seeing no ill effects, pulled round a scabbard attached to his belt. Two passers-by, noticing the fracas, hurried past so as not to get involved. James was just in time to see the Irish ring dagger thrusting at him as he flung out his arm. There was a clink of metal hitting the pavement and James pounded along the side street, ducking between two parked cars in the dark, his heart thudding from the unfamiliar exertion.

There was silence. The rush of blood to James's brain was telling him he had to get back to his own car, depress the door locks and call the police. Mahoney must have gone off his head.

James scuttled into a shop doorway and peered round the corner. Deserted! But he waited for at least five minutes to make sure. Then, taking a deep breath he raced back, keys in hand, pressed the remote and threw himself in the seat.

Declan sprang out from behind the car and grasped the driver's door with his left hand. As the two men tugged with all their strength, the Irishman wedged in his knee and black suede boot. The gap was just wide enough. Declan's right arm lifted and the Irish ring dagger plunged into its target's jaw.

James's searing shriek attracted the attention of a motorcyclist who slewed over and dismounted. Declan broke off the attack and, sheathing his weapon, fled back in the direction of Drury Lane. Once inside the Theatre Royal he ignored all bystanders, slunk through the backstage complex to his dressing room and locked himself in.

Dan, Sally and stage manager Duncan Frith had just completed a search of the building, enlisting the help of other actors and technical staff as they combed the dressing rooms and administrative suite without success. They had even gone through the elaborate ghostly complex beneath the stage calling the actor's name. Now Declan was back in his fortress of his own accord, they were at a loss what to do next.

Julia was inconsolable. On a chair in the front office with Dandy Miles at her side the actress sat mopping her eyes and nose.

'Give 'im a day or two', Dandy was saying, 'he'll be right as rain.'

Julia gnawed her lips and took her mobile out of her bag. She cleared her throat, saw that Dan was within earshot, selected the number and croaked:

'Is that *Dr Raymond*?'

'Julia?' Stence answered, 'Whatever's the matter?'

'Can you come down to the front office? Something's happened.'

'I'll be right there.'

Stence, still in shrink attire but without her tinted glasses, had been pushing out through the swing doors, not wanting to sniff the stars or bathe in their reflected glory. Now she raced back to catch Dan's voice booming above the throng:

'*I don't give a fuck!! Get her back here!*'

'She's, here Dan,' Julia told him.

'Dr Raymond? Right, well we actually have a case for you.' Dan's tone carried both disgust and fury. 'See if you can do anything, can you. He's either stoned or he thinks he's still in the fucking play.'

They marched her through the theatre towards Declan's star dressing room. There Loxley pointed and everybody except Stence withdrew to a safe distance. She could hear Sally pleading: 'We should really call the Saint John people down here Danno - he needs medical treatment.'

Stence knocked softly and, finding no response, bent down to look in the keyhole. Her eye met another eye. She stood away from the door: it scanned who she was and she heard the sound of unlocking fortresses.

She walked in and the door was locked behind her. There was a strong whiff of alcohol. The dressing mirror bulbs were lit, and a candle burned on the worktop next to Julia's mascot. The portrait of Kean as Overreach, hair flying and eyes tormented, graced one wall. Beneath it there was a metal spider, a silver hip flask, a glass full of Jameson's whisky, a newspaper – the *Herald*.

The occupant himself was standing at the back of the room, gripping one arm with the other. His black velvet Hamlet costume was stained on the shoulder with liquid.

Don't look at him, she thought. *Sit on the floor so as not to offer a threat*. There was a futon mattress. She sat on it.

'There was this book I wanted to write,' she began calmly, 'called *The Actor with the Bottle*. Could have been about you. But then I thought, no, that's not very original, is it. Everybody interviews actors. Been done. There's this *other* book, though, much more significant, that nobody has ever written, so far as I know. In this other book, I don't interview *the actor*. I interview the *characters*. I talk to the people who inhabit his frame when he is working. Because I think that symbiosis is the closest relationship known to human beings. What do you think?'

It was a rhetorical question. She did not look up or expect a response. She went on:

'An actor dies a thousand deaths. But they don't all belong to him. Take our Ned, for example.'

She moved her head in the direction of Kean's portrait.

'He died as Richard III. I wasn't there, but I know for a fact he did die. He died as Richard. He died as Othello. He died as Hamlet. But before he died as all these people, *he breathed life into them*. He conjured Shakespeare off the dead page. Each time, he gave up part of his soul. And I should have given *anything* to talk to those characters, getting them to improvise in "Shakespeak". Because I believe they could have told us something important, about us, about the human race and the human mind. It would have been worth the risk.'

Declan had sat down.

'I'm only a writer,' Stence said. 'I can't do what you do. I just put the words on the page. I can't make those words flesh. I can't do that. You can. You did it tonight.'

She thought she heard chuckling and feeling very slightly piqued looked round at him. Declan's head was bowed. His arms were resting on his knees and his shoulders were shaking, but he wasn't laughing: far from it. She went over to him, kneeling down by his chair. She wanted more than anything to touch him, to hug him tight, but stopped herself.

'I know what happened to you,' she whispered, 'and it's OK, because Kean had a total eclipse as well, and he came back. Look at him as Overreach - they thought he was mad and possessed by the Devil, but he came back from that, didn't he?'

Declan raised his face towards her. She thought she was ready for anything but she was shocked. He looked like a man who had been in a war, utterly broken and defeated. His eyes were ringed and filled with tears. All the piercing blue magic of them had gone out, leaving only shadows. He shook his head.

'I can't get out,' he said. 'I've tried. It keeps –' his voice choked off and he made a rotating gesture with his index finger.

Stence grieved for him, but what could she do? Psychology she had studied all her life, but she knew nothing of psychotherapy, nothing of psychiatry, nothing of the talk-down skills of hostage negotiation. There *had* to be a way to reach this man, to make a connection. She didn't have much time.

She searched in her bag and her pockets, felt her handkerchief and her inhaler, and pulled out a folded sheet of paper to show the actor. But Declan had already got out of his seat and disappeared into his bathroom annex.

She looked over at the worktop as she imagined she saw something moving, a trick of the candlelight.

She stood up to look at the antique bear she had brought into the theatre. What a strange dilapidated object it was: an animal shape, wooden, carved, with small ears on the side of its head and sewn into a pelt. It might not be a bear at all. It might once have had a tail and been a monkey.

She walked over to the imposing portrait of Kean and unfolded the tribute poem in her hand. She knew it by heart, but it might be better to let Declan read it. He was the bloody actor. Maybe it would stir some memory inside him, something to hold on to in the chaos that had become of his identity. Sometimes poetry could do that where ordinary words could not – reach inside a person.

She was still examining the painting when she heard a noise and turned to look over her shoulder.

She was just in time to see the eyes, which were white with tiny black pupils. The wolf in Hamlet's clothing.

He grabbed her arms, pulling the bands from her wrists, and the Irish ring dagger blade wrapped round them. The pain shot through her and she fell, sliding down the front of his costume onto the floor.

He sat her gently against the wall and squatted on the floor looking at her. There was no malice. Indeed he seemed quite concerned. She had once heard of a mad painter who tried to sever his own ear to bring him back to reality. Perhaps this was that.

The arterial blood was dark red and there was a lot of it. She tried to press her wrists against herself, but he pulled them away. She began to wheeze and choke, gasping for breath, and knew she was on the edge of absolute panic. She had mastered her asthma years ago by learning to exhale, and she did this now to stop herself hyperventilating. *Breath out, one, two three, four, breath in. Breath out, one, two, three, four, breath in.*

Several minutes went by like this. Declan did not move. He watched her, like a small boy watching an animal die in the road, not attempting to interfere with nature.

Pain and terror had been the fulcrum of Stence's work as a writer. She knew that they conferred certain advantages on the brain. Right now, her mind was a crystal. She brought her breathing under control and looked steadily into the white wolf eyes. If she screamed, Loxley and the others would try to force the door, but that would simply trigger more violence in here. It was probably too late, anyway.

With one nearly lifeless wrist she reached for the piece of paper that had dropped down beside her. She couldn't grasp it but flicked it with her fingers towards Declan, or the person who used to be Declan.

He picked it up and opened the sheet but the pinholes of his vision could make nothing of it. So she softly recited the lines herself. It took a couple of minutes but it was easier than she thought, as she was quite comfortable, sitting there dying with her soul mate. She even smiled at the puns.

TO EDMUND KEAN

I wasn't there the nights he died
As Richard drunk with all his wounds
His arms out parrying the blows.
I wasn't there when Harlequin had to

Tumble and jest though his boy was dead,
When Overreach went off his head
And the pit rose
And the house brought down
And they gave him the clap
In London Town. I wasn't there.

I wasn't there to see him make
Those roles real and those monsters men.
I wasn't there when he wrung their hearts
As the noble Moor with his pagan grief
Or when he seared their scorn away
From Shylock's raped humanity.

When fellow thespians declaimed
Their classic points with pomp and poise
I wasn't there, and yet one hears
He took them by their coxcombs' ears
And rubbed their noses in their work
And wiped the sneers from critics' faces
Staining their copy with their tears.

I wasn't there when he sweated wine
Or when, engorged with spite and sore,
He fell in taverns with the Wolves
As dissolute and drunk as they
And died depraved at forty-four.

I do regret being born too late
To see the mark on Ned Kean's brow
Where heaven's fire left its brand.
But under that black Richmond slab
In the church of Mary Magdalene
There lies a sacred skeleton
Who lived and breathed as any man

Yet held the lightning in his hand.
God bless the stage he went upon
God bless him now that he is gone
And may he rest, if not in peace,
In glory and in genius.

Declan had listened intently. He leaned towards her and examined her face, seeming to search for some connection. She blew up at her fringe as she was hot, so then he carefully pulled off her wig, straightened her hair and gently placed his lips against her forehead, whispering something inaudible. Stencie thought it might be '*Helen, my Helen.*' Then he got up and unlocked the door. Gesturing towards Stence for the benefit of the waiting mob, he pushed past them and vanished in the direction of the stage.

Before most of the crew left for the night, they had struck the final set and replaced it with the opening scenery for Act One Scene One of the next day's performance. Elsinore Castle, and the guard platform.

The rope hanging down from the gridiron was what Declan had had in mind. It seemed to represent a kind of closure. He jumped onto the platform, tested the rope for its certainty and began climbing.

Despite his dissolute lifestyle the 42-year-old actor was strong for his small frame. He reached the gridiron, pulled up the rope and tied a noose in the end. Then he placed it round his neck and hanged himself, the rope swaying and creaking, swinging from side to side with an ever decreasing momentum.

Loxley and Sally were the first to arrive on the scene, and they stopped in their tracks but said nothing. There was very little that anyone could say.

The paramedics in their luminous green jackets could do nothing for the suicide, and one simply entered '*D.O.A.*'(dead on arrival) on his clipboard docket beneath Mahoney's name. The ambulance rushed Stencie Smith to the Royal Free, where she was found to have suffered major organ failure and medics fought with her to save her life, the doctors versus the poet.

Twenty minutes away, James Mayne Young woke up in accident and emergency, his face stitched, asking what they had done with his St Genesius pendant.

Dan Loxley remained in the auditorium for a long time. Being a man of theatre through and through he felt the need for some sort of tribute. He asked a technician who had remained behind to play one of the taped voiceovers of Hamlet's private thoughts, that they had used so successfully during the performance to replace stage whispers.

Loxley had the famous 'To be or not to be...' soliloquy fed through the theatre's PA system. What else?

The disembodied voice had belonged to Declan Mahoney. Perhaps it still did.

'*For who would bear the whips and scorns of time,*
The oppressor's wrong, the proud man's contumely,
The pangs of dispriz'd love, the law's delay,
The insolence of office, and the spurns

That patient merit of th'unworthy takes,
When he himself might his quietus make
With a bare bodkin? Who would fardels bear,
To grunt and sweat under a weary life,
But that the dread of something after death,
The undiscovered country, from whose bourn
No traveller returns, puzzles the will,
And makes us rather bear those ills we have,
Than fly to others that we know not of?'

Julia Lord came and stood in the auditorium to pay her own respects to a flawed man, a selfish lover, but an actor of most extraordinary gifts. She could not have done this alone. John Padgett's arm was around her shoulders. Her partner had come the moment she called, as true partners usually do.

Julia looked in his face and said there was one thing she had to attend to before they could go home.

She went into Declan's dressing room, picked up Fardels Bear and dropped him in the metal waste bin. Then she threw in the lighted candle and watched the whole thing burn, giving off small coloured flares like minerals trapped in lighted coal.

END

Lightning Source UK Ltd.
Milton Keynes UK
UKOW02f0502011114

240924UK00002B/15/P

9 781785 100154